Kane:
I am Alpha

Nicky Charles

Edited by Jan Gordon
Line edits by Moody Edits

Cover Design by Jazer Designs
Cover images used under license from Shutterstock.com
Paw print and wolf head logo
Copyright © Doron Goldstein, Designer

ISBN: 978-1-989058-24-4

Dedication

To all my fans whose avid support of this series continues
to overwhelm me each and every day!

I would also like to dedicate this book to Mark Coker, the
'Alpha' of Smashwords. It was his vision of an
independent publishing platform for authors that made it
possible for me and numerous others to share our books
with the world. Without him, it is doubtful you would be
reading this book!

Acknowledgements

Thank you to those who helped cross-check facts and who read the rough drafts. Your feedback was invaluable.

I'd also like to give a special shout-out to Jennifer Barner who went above and beyond by finding important passages in The Mating that had to be addressed in this tale!

Foreword

This novella was written in response to the ongoing requests to hear Kane's side of The Mating, the original Law of the Lycans story. Please be aware it took considerable time and extensive cajoling to get him to agree to an interview. As he informed me on more than one occasion, an Alpha is a very busy individual and any spare time he has would be better spent with his mate and pups rather than humouring an author.

(Hmph! For the record, I was quite proud of my self-restraint during such moments when I bit my tongue rather than remind him that *I* am the person who created him. However, Kane might be surprised at the retribution I dish out to him in future stories!)

On that note, I'd like to state that any anomalies between this text and previously written stories are solely the result of Kane's absent-minded replies to my questions rather than a lack of fact checking on my part. Please direct any complaints towards him and not me!

The Alpha is the designated leader and all other pack members look to him for guidance. He assumes his title either by default from his sire or by earning the position through a political voting process. On rare occasions a leadership challenge might occur which usually results in a fight to the death, however, this is less common in modern times. Political manoeuvring, even small campaigns within the pack, are becoming more and more the norm when determining leadership.

Once an Alpha assumes his role, the mantle of responsibility weighs heavily...

Source: The Book of the Law

Prologue

Kane stood, hands in his pockets, idly listening to the discussion around him. It was Zack's birthday and they were celebrating the Alpha's special day with a night out in a city about an hour from home. Having finished dinner at a local restaurant with the requisite cake and song, they were now going to see a movie. Three of Zack's daughters were present and strongly advocating for seeing a chic flick while their husbands wanted to watch a zombie movie.

"Ryne, which one do you think we should see?" Zoe appealed to Ryne, her father's other co-Beta.

Ryne shrugged. "Makes no difference to me. What about you, Marla?"

Marla, Ryne's girlfriend, hung on his arm. "It doesn't matter to me, as long as it's dark and we get a private corner."

Chloe, Zack's youngest daughter made a gagging motion behind Marla's back and Kane couldn't help but chuckle.

Helen, the girls' mother, clapped her hands. "Enough. It's your father's birthday. He gets to decide." She turned and smiled at her mate.

"What? I actually get a say?" His comment was ironic since, as pack Alpha, his word was law.

"Of course, you get to pick, Dad. We all know you have excellent taste when it comes to movies."

Phoebe smiled and tried to lead him towards the chic flick.

Kane tuned out the discussion and began to study his surroundings. It was more crowded than usual likely due to the heatwave that gripped the area. The dark, air-conditioned theatre offered some temporary relief from the mid-summer warmth. Couples, families, groups of teens; they brushed past where he stood, momentarily blocking the view of the movie posters that decorated the walls and causing the smell of popcorn and melted butter to swirl throughout the space.

One particular scent caught his attention and he began to search for the source only pausing when his gaze landed on a gathering of young women. They were Lycans, though their t-shirts and denim, the favoured garb of teens, allowed them to blend in with the crowd.

He cocked his head. The movie theatre was on the edge of the Rock Valley pack's territory so it wasn't surprising to run into others of his kind. They certainly presented no threat. Still, there was something about the group that kept his attention riveted to them.

They didn't seem to notice him which spoke poorly of their skills. He frowned in annoyance. Instead of laughing and giggling about the actor pictured in one of the movie posters, they should be attending to their surroundings. He decided some instruction at the Academy would do them good. While he was a strong proponent of peaceful co-existence with humans, young Lycans needed to remember their heritage.

About to turn away, the group of girls moved and he noticed another member who had, thus far, been hidden from view. For some reason, the sight of her caused him to freeze in place, his breath catching in his throat, his blood heating in his veins. His inner wolf immediately awakened and fixed its attention on the female with an intensity he'd never experienced before.

She was of average height with rich brown hair, deep green eyes and a warm smile. Exactly what attracted him, he wasn't sure. Pretty but not stunning, her appearance wouldn't normally garner such a reaction from him. Maybe it was the fact that she was quieter than the others or perhaps it was the composed way she held herself.

He narrowed his eyes and inhaled, trying to sort through the various scents and isolate hers.

Talk to her, his wolf urged.

He actually stepped towards her when someone grabbed his arm.

"Come on, Kane. Dad's decided on that historical film." Chloe handed him a container of popcorn and he absently smiled his thanks, his attention still focused on the girl.

Who was she? He watched as she ate a bit of popcorn then licked her lips. Damn but he wanted to taste her, to press his lips to hers. He wished she would look his way. Would she feel the same pull between them that he was experiencing?

"Hey Kane, quit day-dreaming." Ryne nudged him. "What are you thinking about? Plotting how to get Zack to let you drive his new toy?"

"Er...yeah." He forced himself to look away from the girl and grasped the excuse his half-brother had provided. "Helen couldn't have picked a better present than that truck."

"Yep. But if anyone gets to drive it besides Zack, it will be me."

"As if that would ever happen." He couldn't resist glancing over his shoulder one more time. Of course, Ryne had to notice.

"Found yourself a bit of eye-candy, I see." Ryne flicked his eyes over the group of girls. "Too young for my taste but pretty."

"Don't let Marla hear you say that," he warned, thankful his brother hadn't realized it was one particular individual in the group that had captured his attention. The idea of another male looking at the girl made his inner wolf bristle.

"Marla's in the washroom," Ryne pointed out. "Besides, I know how to keep her sweet."

Kane laughed and followed his packmates into the movie but, when the evening was over, he had no recollection what the film was about. The faint lingering scent of a brown-haired female had been much more captivating than the actors on the screen.

Chapter 1

A massive wolf stood on an outcropping of rock, head lifted proudly as the sun glinted off its jet-black fur. Behind it, white clouds dotted a bright blue sky creating the perfect backdrop for such an animal. It was a picture that begged to be captured and saved for posterity. Of course, artistic merit was of no importance to the creature. There were more important things to be concerned about, namely guarding the pack's territory.

The wolf was intent on surveying the area, keen amber eyes skimming over all that lay before it, noting minute changes that most would overlook. This was the animal's domain and it knew every inch of the land like a lover. They were as one; the land whispering to the wolf, revealing its secrets, providing shelter and sustenance. In exchange, the wolf guarded it with a ferocity that was not to be denied.

Small meadows, a stream that merged with a river and eventually a lake, tall pines, broad maples, oaks and cottonwoods, distant ravines and scrubby underbrush; it spread as far as the eye could see. The shades of grey and blue and green and brown mixed and blended in perfect harmony while the occasional bright dots of colour formed by wild flowers and birds provided areas of contrast. It was an intriguing yet soothing palette that filled the animal with contentment.

Yes, the forest was more than the wolf's home; it was a living breathing entity, his heritage, a gift to be passed on to future generations so that they too could thrive, enjoying and protecting the gifts of nature. The wolf and land needed each other. If one faltered, so did the other.

Of course, a wolf also needed a mate and he had yet to find a suitable one within the territory. Well...there had been one belonging to another pack. The female's image shimmered before him only to fade. They had not met but he'd felt an instant attraction to her. She'd been young and beautiful and he could see her bearing many fine pups to build the pack. Would they ever meet again though? That would be for the gods to decide.

A scent drifted by on the breeze. The wolf's nostrils flared as he inhaled deeply then frowned. Two others were coming and he turned his head, amber eyes searching for signs of movement. It was his half-brother and a female from the pack. He made no effort to move and greet them, instead waiting for them to approach. He was on duty and wouldn't leave his post.

"There he is!" Ryne, his brother, called out.

"Hello, Kane!" The female, Marla, clutched Ryne's hand as if the ground were too rough for her to traverse on her own.

The wolf narrowed his eyes in annoyance. Marla was an anomaly, more comfortable in her human skin than in her wolf form, enjoying the comforts of civilization over the rugged beauty of nature. She had her reasons, but he often wondered if a bit more effort on her part wouldn't make life easier for everyone. Indulging her tried his patience at times, especially when she attempted to play him and his brother off each other. Thankfully, she seemed to have settled recently.

"You make a pretty picture standing there like that," Ryne joked.

The word 'pretty' had the wolf swishing its tail.

Ryne liked nothing better than to tease him over his preference for a trimmed appearance. An unkempt beard and longer hair were Ryne's choice, in keeping with his artistic bent or so he said. The man was a photographer, a damned good one though telling him so would only inflate his already bloated self-esteem.

Not that he and Ryne didn't get along. As half-brothers, they were closer than most full-blooded siblings, a harsh upbringing had formed a strong bond between them. They were also incredibly similar in appearance, however, even as pups their personalities had set them apart. Everyone had always said he was the calm, logical one while Ryne was wild and wicked.

"We've been taking pictures."

Marla's announcement drew the wolf's attention. He watched as she sat down.

She flicked her long, blond hair over her shoulder managing to lounge elegantly despite the fact she was perched on a log. "I'm going to help Ryne arrange another exhibit. Now that I've been promoted at Bastian's I'll have more say on the scheduling of art shows."

"You'd make a great picture, Kane." Ryne raised his camera.

"That's a wonderful idea." Marla clapped her hands. "Kane, you're so handsome, everyone will be fawning over a picture of you."

"I thought I was the handsome one?" Ryne quirked a brow at her and she laughed.

"You're a sexy, dashing devil and you know it, Ryne Taylor."

Ryne bent and gave her a thorough kiss. "And don't you forget it." He turned towards his brother and began to focus the camera. "Give me a smile, Kane."

A growl from his intended subject caused Ryne

to pause. "Now don't go all wolfie on me, Kane. I know you don't want any humans to see pictures of Lycans. This would just be for family."

He hesitated and Ryne pressed his point.

"It could be a Christmas present for Helen. You know she dotes on you."

He cocked his head and then sighed, giving his permission.

"Great." Ryne quickly began snapping pictures from various angles.

Finally tired, the wolf yawned and shifted to human form. "That's enough, Ryne. I'm supposed to be working not acting like some pin-up boy."

Marla grinned. "And a fine pin-up boy you'd be."

"Again with praising Kane?" Ryne scowled. "It seems you need a lesson on which brother you belong to."

Marla stood and pressed herself to him. "I can't wait."

Kane rolled his eyes. "Why don't you two get a room?"

"Because Marla already has an apartment," Ryne winked. "You must be getting senile. You were the one who helped her get it."

"Senile? You're the older brother." He raised one brow. "You might want to get Marla to pluck those grey hairs."

Ryne caught himself in the act of raising a hand to his temple. "I don't have grey hair."

"Of course you don't." Kane then winked at Marla. "Right, Marla?"

She laughed and shook her head. "You two, always joking."

"It's what brothers do best." He grinned reflecting on the many escapades they'd shared over the years.

The sound of a vehicle caught his attention and he turned to stare towards a distant road. "Looks like Zack is on his way home."

Ryne glanced towards where he was looking. "Yep. He's really enjoying that new truck. He guards it like a hawk. I haven't even had a chance to drive it yet."

"Really? I took it for a spin yesterday. I even had a chance to look under the hood." Kane couldn't resist the gentle gibe. "Of course, I *am* his favourite."

"Favourite? Ha!" Ryne rolled his eyes. "More like he took pity on you for being the lowly younger brother."

"Boys, please!" Marla stepped in front of Ryne and slid her hands over his chest and then up to his neck where she linked her fingers. "Your bickering is hilarious, but I really think we should be going." She stood on tiptoe and nipped at Ryne's chin.

Kane looked away, the public displays between these two were a bit much. Zack's truck was still in view, a streak of black and silver. "He seems to be going awfully fast."

"He probably can't wait to get home to Helen." Marla nuzzled against Ryne. "Let's head back to my apartment. I can check you for grey hair."

"In a minute." Ryne shrugged her off and stepped closer to Kane. "Zack never speeds."

"No, he doesn't." Kane shifted restlessly, a sense of unease coming over him. "I have a bad feeling about this."

"Me, too."

Now the two brothers stood shoulder to shoulder,

watching their Alpha take one curve and then another at what seemed to be increasing speed until trees obscured him from view.

"Come on, Ryne." Marla swatted at the air. "There are too many bugs here."

"Yeah," Ryne glanced at her and then back to where the truck had disappeared from sight. "I'll take you—"

A distant sound interrupted him, like the crashing of metal and then a loud bang. Both men gave a start and began to run.

"Zack!"

Chapter 2

Kane put his arm around Helen's shoulders, offering her what support he could as they stood by the fresh grave. It was located on a bluff overlooking the territory Zack had ruled for so long, the view showcasing the land in all its majesty. The pack could take comfort in knowing their Alpha was still watching over them, his spirit in the breeze that wound through the trees and dipped into the valleys.

That comfort was hard to feel at the moment, though. The dappled shade that danced over the gravestone reminded him of the tears that had fallen on the day of the accident. Breaking the news to the pack had been difficult. Watching Helen weep had been even harder. She'd needed no one to inform her what had happened, of course. The bond with her mate had let her know the minute he'd died, and she'd collapsed, clutching her chest as sobs shuddered through her.

Even now, she struggled to recover from that fateful day.

"I feel so dead inside. All I want to do is curl up in a ball and never get up again." Helen's voice was flat, emotionless, as if she had no energy left even to mourn.

He nodded. Zack had been her blood-bonded mate, his death akin to her own.

One stray tear made its way down her cheek. She made no move to wipe it away instead letting the symbol of her sorrow slowly evaporate into the wind. It was fitting, the tear returning to the atmosphere, becoming one with the life force of the earth just as her mate had done.

"You're strong, Helen. It's hard but Zack would want you to continue on." Kane knew his words were meaningless platitudes but it was all he had to offer. He was floundering himself, feeling lost, unsure of the next step. Helen had already said she wouldn't continue as Alpha female which meant the leadership of the pack was up in the air. Wolves needed to know who was Alpha to feel secure. Thankfully, the issue would be decided tonight at the vote.

Today was the last official day of grieving according to Lycan tradition. It had been a week since the day Zack's brakes had failed and his vehicle had plunged off the road, crashing down the rocky cliff killing him. He and Ryne, as co-Betas, had officiated at the departing ceremony which had been held the next day. It had been difficult, Zack having been like a father to them for much of their life.

Now Kane stood with Helen as she placed a bouquet of flowers near the headstone, her last official act as Alpha female. Ryne waited nearby, arms folded, his face clouded. Kane studied his brother with concern. Ever since the crash, Ryne had been troubled. Well, they all had been, naturally, but this was something more. The man was surly, going off on his own or spending time with Marla. While those two were a couple, Ryne had never been reticent about his activities, always speaking openly about his affair with her. Now there was a secretive air about him, as if he were hiding something. It had taken considerable cajoling on Helen's part to get Ryne to even accompany them to the grave today.

Kane decided to try and talk to Ryne once more before the meeting. They'd both be vying for the Alpha position. As siblings they'd often been in good-natured competition with each other, and while this was more serious than a one on one basketball game, the vote shouldn't cause a problem between them. No, there was something else bothering his brother. With a thoughtful nod, he shifted his attention back to Helen who was speaking again.

"I shouldn't have given him that truck. Why did I think it would be a good birthday present for him?"

"It was what he wanted," Ryne spoke up, his voice gruff. "He'd been talking about replacing his old junker for ages."

"Well, his junker had perfect brakes." Helen twisted a tissue in her hands. "I can't help but feel this is my fault."

Ryne shot a look at Kane, the kind of silent communication they'd always used, almost as if they knew each other's thoughts.

A hint of a smile tugged at the corner of Kane's mouth. It was like old days, the two of them in tune with each other.

Ryne raised a brow. Should they tell her?

He nodded. "Helen, it wasn't your fault."

"That's what everyone keeps saying but *I* bought the truck. *I* handed him the keys. I'm even the one who called him and told him to hurry home for supper that day." Her voice cracked, a distant, haunted look coming over her as she relived the fateful day.

Ryne shook his head. "No, we mean it wasn't *your* fault. It was someone else's."

She looked between them, her brows knit together. "I don't understand."

"It could have been a flaw in the material," Kane began, "a hole in a hose that allowed fluid to leak out..."

"But we suspect someone actually tampered with the brakes." Ryne finished the explanation, his dark brows knit together.

"No!" Helen gasped, her face paling. "Who would do that?"

"We have no idea, do we Kane?" Ryne gave him an odd look.

Kane frowned once again unable to discern the vibes coming from his brother. "No, we have no suspects. Zack was well-liked."

"He was. You must be mistaken. Tampering with the brakes makes no sense." Helen's thoughts seemed to be racing as she tried to make sense of the revelation. "Could it have been random vandalism? But when would there have been an opportunity?"

Ryne shrugged, a muscle working in his jaw.

"Zach didn't let anyone near that truck." Kane pointed out.

"We can't tell the police about your suspicions." Helen rung her hands. "They might ask questions we can't answer. Zack worked so hard to keep our pack under the human radar."

"Our thoughts exactly. The risk is too great. That's why we sat on the information." Kane ran his hand through his hair, frustrated that they had to let the matter go.

"The authorities have already concluded it was human error." Ryne shoved his hands in his pockets. "Nothing can bring my Zack back regardless of the cause." Helen took a deep breath and stepped forward to place her hand on the headstone, slowly tracing the name carved on it. "He's gone and no one will ever replace him." Her voice trailed off, then she pressed her lips together and seemed to gather some inner strength. "As much as I want to avenge his death, Zack would say the good of the pack comes first."

"I'll do my best to make sure the person responsible is held accountable." Ryne jutted his chin, eyes narrowed as he stared out over the land below.

"We both will." Kane began to lead Helen back to the car.

"You're such good boys." Helen held out her arm, reaching for Ryne so that she had one man on either side of her. "I'm so lucky to have you to lean on. You're like the sons I never had."

"We're the lucky ones. You took us in," Kane began but Helen shook her head.

"Of course, we took you in. You needed a stable family."

"And with four daughters already, you needed two more teenagers running around the house." Ryne added.

"You did liven things up." Helen patted his arm.

"And I tried to keep him in line," Kane smiled at memories of their antics.

Ryne didn't respond.

The drive back to the house was completed in silence. Kane glanced in the rear-view mirror. Ryne was staring out the window, brows lowered, mouth tight. Helen was lost in thought as well, no doubt mourning her lost mate.

As for himself, he was considering what would happen at the pack meeting tonight. A new Alpha would be chosen, but who? An Alpha assumed his title either by default from his sire or by earning the position through a political voting process. On rare occasions a leadership challenge might occur, a fight to the death, but that wouldn't be the case here. Political manoeuvring, even small campaigns within the pack were more the norm.

15

He doubted any of Zack's daughters would throw their hat in the ring. Not that female Alphas didn't exist—there were a few out there—however, Zack's girls had never shown an interest in leadership. No, it would likely be a vote between himself and Ryne. As co-Betas, one of them was the most logical choice. John, another pack member, would also be a good candidate as well. He was a solid, level-headed sort though he didn't exude the dominance needed to keep the pack in line on his own. Of course, that might come with assuming the mantel of responsibility. You never knew what you were capable of until the opportunity arose.

Brother against brother; who would the Council of Elders favour? While it was the final vote of the pack that determined the outcome, the opinion of the Council could often sway the decision. If he was chosen, he was prepared. Already the idea filled his inner wolf with excitement. It was a strong, clever animal, loyal and aware of its duty. The others in the pack acknowledged its power, showing it the deference and respect an Alpha deserved.

"Let me out here." Ryne spoke, jerking Kane out of his reverie.

He pulled over.

"Are you sure, Ryne?" Helen looked around. "We're near the lake and it's quite a hike to the pack house."

"I'm heading to town to see Marla." Ryne was already opening the door.

"Oh." Helen's one word spoke volumes. She didn't approve of Marla and never had.

Ryne either didn't pick up on her disapproval or didn't care. "I'll see you at the meeting tonight." He climbed out of the car and slammed the door, then stood on the side of the road. His posture was stiff, his hands fisted.

Kane drove away, very aware that Ryne was glaring at him.

Helen apparently picked up on the vibe as well. "What's bothering him?"

He shrugged not wanting to add to her worries. "I've no idea. You know how he can be; some little thing probably ticked him off this morning. He'll get over it."

"No, ever since Zack...passed away, Ryne's been acting differently." Helen bit her lip and then slid him a sideways glance. "Do you think it's the upcoming vote that has him concerned?"

"Could be." He answered cautiously, wondering how Helen might be feeling about the vote. After all, someone was going to be taking over the position her mate had held for years.

"Ryne's older than you. Some might think that's a reason to choose him over you for the position of Alpha."

"I've thought of that." He nodded while his inner wolf frowned.

"I'm not so sure though." Helen clasped her hands in her lap. "Ryne's a good boy."

He laughed at the description. "Hardly a boy."

Helen shook her head. "You know what I mean. Both of you will always be boys to me."

A smile tugged at the corner of his mouth. And no matter how old he was, Helen would always be able to have him quaking in his boots as she brandished her wooden spoon.

"Anyway, as I was saying. Ryne's a good...man." She shot him a look. "But so are you."

"Thanks."

"And I think you would make a better Alpha."

"Really?" He looked at her in surprise. Helen had never shown either of them favouritism growing up despite the fact he and Ryne often joked about it.

"Your brother is very similar to you but with a rougher edge. His wolf is smart and powerful yet wilder, quick to react without thinking. Our pack is big and influential. We need a cool head at the helm and that's you."

He'd been thinking along the same lines. "Well—"

"And don't think I'm unaware that he's a lusty creature as well. He's had more than his fair share of women."

"That doesn't mean he couldn't be a good Alpha." He felt he had to point that out.

"True, but hear me out." She pursed her lips before speaking. "Lately, he seems to have settled on Marla and that's a cause for some concern."

He nodded slowly, knowing what she meant. He, Ryne and Marla had grown up together and, like them, she'd always been on the outside looking in though for very different reasons. He and Ryne had been transient members due to their rocky childhood whereas Marla had always lived in the pack yet never seemed to fit in. She'd confided to him once that she was only three-quarters Lycan and, as a result, felt like she didn't belong. He was sure no one suspected her secret and, if they did, they wouldn't care but she'd never bought into his reasoning.

The real problem was that she lacked the basic pack instinct and understanding of social interaction. It was the only explanation for how often she aggravated others. He knew she didn't do it on purpose and had often suggested she shift to her wolf form more often to improve her relationship with the creature. Her inner wolf could teach her quite a bit, he'd pointed out. She'd laughed, saying she knew all she needed to know of the beast.

"Marla isn't Alpha female material." Helen continued to explain her reasoning. "I've held the position for a long time and I know for a fact it's no walk in the park. There's a lot to be done behind the scenes and Marla isn't up to it."

"You could teach her." Why he was playing devil's advocate, he had no idea.

Helen shook her head. "If Ryne becomes Alpha and chooses Marla as his mate, she'll have a lot of responsibilities, none of which she'll want to learn. Can you picture her helping to get the house ready for delegates from other packs and preparing meals? Or listening to the pack members when they have problems with their pups? Oh no, she'll want to sit around looking elegant, buffing her nails while waiting for someone to serve her bonbons! And that's when she's not spending pack money." Helen's cheeks began to turn pink as she warmed to her topic. "Plus. she'll be able to influence the decisions Ryne makes and you know she has no love of the land. When she heard about that offer from the oil company, she was all over it trying to tell Zack he needed to sign the contract and not to worry about the environmental impact."

Kane tightened his grip on the steering wheel, feeling a knot forming in his stomach. If Ryne was chosen as Alpha, things could get dicey. Ryne would keep him as Beta, surely, and he'd be able to guide him. Hopefully. Ryne could be a bull-headed bastard at times...

Chapter 3

The meeting room in the lower level of the pack house was crowded, almost all members of eligible age having turned out for the leadership vote. A number of Lycans had gathered around the front where Kane stood, offering him support and giving advice about how to deal with the debate.

Nodding absentmindedly, he surreptitiously wiped his palms on the legs of his pants. His bout of nerves surprised him. He wanted this job. Badly. He hadn't realized how much until now. Maybe he should have spent more time this past week campaigning but he'd been busy dealing with the crash investigation and trying to keep things running smoothly. Ryne hadn't been much help, either, disappearing for long periods of time doing who knew what.

He scanned the room for his brother. There was no sign of him despite the fact the meeting would start soon. Typical. Ryne followed the rules only when they suited his purpose.

His inner wolf stirred restlessly wanting the meeting to start. The animal was being unexpectedly unruly today and he was struggling to keep it in line. It sensed the potential to rise in the pack and some kind of testosterone surge seemed to be taking place. If the vote didn't go in his favour, he'd be hard pressed to deal with the disappointment. There was nothing wrong with the Beta position; he'd been content to fulfill those duties but now he wanted more. Trying to distract himself, he looked around the room identifying those gathered.

Of course, the Council of Elders was seated at the front to the side of the podium. The rest of the pack occupied the rows of chairs that filled the room while others stood at the back, leaning against the walls or huddled in groups. He'd known them all for years and considered some to be close friends; how would being Alpha change their relationship? Would he still be included in impromptu gatherings and casual banter? Or would his position change the dynamics? Hopefully not.

He continued his survey of the room. John was near the front with his mate, Carrie. She was expecting their first pup and John had his arms protectively wrapped around her, his hands resting on her belly. She looked up at him, the affection between them undeniable. A twinge of envy passed through Kane and he hoped he'd someday have a relationship like theirs.

With the girl? His wolf chimed in, momentarily distracted from the prospect of being Alpha.

"The one from the movie theatre?" He murmured inwardly. "Not likely. We don't even know who she is."

If you tried, you could find out. A few inquiries, a search of Lycan Link's database; It would yield the information we need. The animal pressed its point.

"If we become Alpha, we won't have time for such nonsense."

Hmm... The wolf frowned, torn between the desire for a mate and the importance of duty.

Kane left the creature to puzzle over the problem and returned to contemplating John. He was a good man. Strong and level-headed.

Perhaps feeling his gaze, John looked up and their eyes met. Kane nodded and so did John. They'd been friends for years and John had assured him earlier in the day he wouldn't be going after the Alpha position.

~~~

"I've got a pup being born soon. I want to concentrate on my family," John said. "The job is yours if you want it, Kane."

"Or it might be Ryne's." He added his brother's name to the conversation.

John gave a one-shouldered shrug. "Perhaps, but I'm voting for you. Ryne's a great guy but too volatile for my liking and I know a lot of others feel the same way."

"Well, we'll have to see how the question period goes. The pack has the opportunity to question the candidates before voting, you know." Inwardly, he was pleased with the vote of confidence.

"You've got this, Kane." John nodded. "You know the Book of the Law cover to cover and you're up to date on all the issues."

"Thanks." He paused, considering something that had been bothering him. "If the vote goes in my favour, would you be interested in the position of co-Beta?"

John pursed his lips thoughtfully. "Yeah, probably. I'll talk it over with Carrie first and let you know."

He gave a satisfied nod and John went on his way.

~~~

Kane hooked his thumbs in his belt loops. He hoped to keep Ryne on as a co-Beta. His brother was good at the job but, if Ryne lost the vote, he might not take it well. Hopefully he wouldn't do something stupid like leaving the pack but it was better to be prepared. Ryne had leadership potential if he only remembered to keep his emotions under control. And speaking of Ryne...

Near the back of the room, a door opened and Kane watched as Ryne entered with Marla. She was looking smug as she clung to his arm whereas Ryne's shoulders were hunched, his face dark as his gaze darted about the room before finally finding its target...him.

The coldness in Ryne's gaze had Kane stiffening. Hatred, aggression; there was no hint of brotherly love about him. Ryne barely acknowledged those around him, several patting him on the back obviously expressing support of him as a candidate. On some level, Kane noted the crowd around Ryne wasn't as big as the one he had around him. It would seem the chance of the vote going in his favour had increased.

Strangely, the realization did nothing to calm his inner wolf. The animal had begun to pace, its hackles rising at Ryne's silent challenge. Without realizing it, he took a half-step towards Ryne, only to pause when Helen caught his arm.

"Behave yourself, Kane." She hissed the warning to him. "People are watching and starting a fight won't win you any votes."

He took a deep breath. She was right. "Sorry." He gave her a crooked smile.

"I don't know what's going on with Ryne," she whispered her concern, "but stay calm and remember you are the best candidate for the job. Our pack needs you."

"Sure." He glanced at Ryne again and then forced himself to look away, noting Helen seemed quite composed given the circumstances. She possessed a strong spirit and he was fortunate to have her on his side.

"Attention. Attention, please." William, a member of the Council stood at the podium, tapping a gavel. "This meeting is now called to order." He waited a moment until every one quieted down. "As you know, we are here to choose our next Alpha. Zack's mate and blood off-spring have abdicated the position so we now open the floor to any and all who wish to be considered for the job."

"I step forward for consideration." Both Kane and Ryne spoke together.

The unplanned unity of speech caused a nervous titter to fill the air. Even though the vote was supposed to be civilized, emotions ran high in the room. Whoever won the vote would need to heal any rifts quickly. A pack divided wouldn't last long.

"Ryne Taylor and Kane Sinclair, your names are allowed to stand." William scanned the crowd. "Is there anyone else?" A heavy silence filled the room as gazes darted about the room looking for a raised hand. A second ticked by and then another. When no one spoke, he banged the gavel. "We have two candidates for consideration."

Those gathered seemed to relax. Knowing two of their own were up for the job, eased the tension. The chance that an outsider could step forward was always a possibility. News of Zack's death had been reported to Lycan Link and an official statement sent out on the Lycan news wires. Given the size and long history of the pack, the tragic event was considered a matter of public interest in the Lycan community. It also meant that any wolf hoping to rise to power knew of the vacancy and could have shown up. Everyone was thankful that hadn't happened.

William consulted his notes. "Following protocol, we will allow time for questioning before the vote. I know many of you have concerns about the push by the oil company that wants permission to do exploratory drilling in part of our territory. As you are aware, they want to buy a large tract or lease it..."

Kane's eyes drifted back to Ryne. Marla was whispering to Ryne, seeming to encourage him but Ryne wasn't reacting well to whatever she said, his scowl deepening.

"Kane, can you answer our first question?" William's voice jerked Kane's attention back to the front.

Damn, what was the question? He had cleared his throat to speak when Ryne suddenly pushed his way to the front.

"He isn't fit or deserving of being Alpha! I issue a challenge!"

A collective gasp filled the room as everyone surged to their feet.

Kane blinked, a red-haze of rage clouding his vision, his wolf taking over.

Our brother has challenged us for leadership, a fight to the death. The animal snarled in rage. *All blood ties are now broken.*

His hands curled into fists and he began to stalk towards his opponent, vaguely aware of Helen, her face pale as she shook her head in denial.

The crowd parted before him, shrinking back as they sensed his mood. Once at the front, he stood facing his challenger, a low rumble rising from his chest, a sound that was echoed by Ryne.

They were evenly matched in size and strength both as humans and as wolves. Indeed, they'd often been mistaken for each other in their younger years, only personality traits and eye-colour separating them.

Both quick and clever, they were a formidable team. But now, now they were dominant males each intent on gaining leadership of the pack. Breathing heavily, material stretched over bunching muscles as the air shimmered around them. Their inner wolves struggled to be released, manipulating the energy around them to bring about a transformation, as low growls filled the air.

"Enough!" William banged the gavel several times, raising his voice as he tried to gain control. "Everyone take their seats. And you two," he looked at Kane and Ryne. "Stand down. I want you on opposite sides of the room while the Council of Elders confers."

Eyes locked on each other, both paused before responding, only respect for the law causing them to move back to neutral corners.

Nervous whispers filled the room as the pack waited to learn what would happen. Kane ignored the sounds around him, his eyes fixed on Ryne. His wolf did not trust the other to stay where he'd been told.

The Council of Elders huddled together, no doubt caught off-guard by this unexpected turn of events. A Council was comprised of retired Alphas and aged members of the pack whose wisdom and experience were considered valuable in guiding the pack and ultimately the Alpha. Not all packs had a council but, given the size of this territory and the number of Lycans involved, it was helpful to have extra input, especially in cases like this.

William left the huddle for a minute to get the Book of the Law. The Council would want to ensure they were following proper procedure for such a grave situation.

Minutes ticked past before the members could be seen nodding. A decision had been reached. As the spokesman, William approached the podium again and took his place. He cleared his throat and then waited for silence. When he had everyone's attention, he began to speak.

"Ryne Taylor has issued a challenge for the leadership of this pack. It is his right, even though highly unusual in these enlightened times." William fixed Ryne with a pointed stare but Ryne didn't flinch. After a beat, William continued. "We now must hear from the other person under consideration as Alpha. Kane Sinclair, do you accept the leadership challenge from your brother or will you step down?"

Even without looking, Kane knew all eyes were focused on him. He could end this now, refuse the challenge and let Ryne take the position, avoiding bloodshed. It was the easy way out, some might even think it was the logical choice. Had that been Ryne's strategy, knowing his brother was the cool headed one?

His inner wolf railed against that choice insisting they were destined to be Alpha. His logical half also expressed doubts especially in light of his conversation with Helen earlier in the day. He looked out over those gathered; packmates, friends. His duty was to the pack and the land they lived on. Ryne was his brother yet the good of all took precedent over family ties.

Slowly, he inhaled and nodded. "I accept."

Pandemonium broke out. Ryne lunged at him, snarling even as others reached out, managing to hold him back. Helen was crying, others stood in shock. Supporters of Ryne started to push and shove those on the other side while William banged his gavel demanding everyone settle down.

By chance, Kane turned his head just in time to see Marla slipping out the back door.

Chapter 4

That night, Kane lay in bed staring at the ceiling. Midsummer heat filled the room, drifting in through the open window, causing a sheen of sweat to slick his skin. He kicked off the covers and folded his arms behind his head. It was his thoughts rather than the heat that was keeping him awake. The challenge had been scheduled for the next day. Well, technically today since it was now well past midnight. He'd yet to fall asleep. By this time tomorrow he'd be Alpha...or not. His feelings were still conflicted on that point.

He watched the passage of the moonlight as it slowly traversed across the wall of his room, skimming over his dresser, slowly illuminating a photo of himself as a youngster with Zack. He was holding a fish and Zack had a hand on his shoulder. He, Ryne and Zack had gone camping together; swimming, fishing, roasting marshmallows.

~~~

"Look Zack. I caught a fish!"

"Good job, Kane. Reel it in slowly." Zack coached him along. "It's a big one. Enough for all three of us for dinner."

"I'll take a picture." Ryne grabbed the camera Helen and Zack had given him.

"I did it! I did it!" He'd held the fish up high, a feeling of pride swelling within him when Zack had placed a hand on his shoulder.

"Way to go, Kane." Ryne had snapped photos while offering praise.

~~~

The sound of their young voices echoed in his head and a bittersweet smile twisted his lips. Those innocent days were gone forever. It was still hard to believe how quickly things had changed.

Trying to distract himself, he brought to mind an image of the brown-haired girl. She always soothed him with her soft smile and deep green eyes. He could picture her standing beside him, her hair blowing gently in the breeze. He'd reach out and tuck the strands behind her ear, then lean down to kiss her...

Right. It was foolish fantasy and he was far too old to be mooning over someone he'd only seen once and had never even spoken to. An Alpha, or at least a potential one, had more weighty things to think about. With a sigh, he let the vision fade.

He ran a hand over his bare chest. There was an ache inside him, a pain over what amounted to a betrayal by his brother. Half-brother to be accurate but they'd never dwelt on that fact. A harsh upbringing had forged a deep bond between them...or so he'd thought.

Their mother, Mindy, had phenomenally bad taste in men. Her relationship with Ryne's father hadn't worked out while his own father was a bastard. They'd never known when they'd be fed, when they'd be on the receiving end of a drunken rage or when they'd wake up to discover they were moving to a new pack. There'd been a few good times but, for the most part, life had been tough. Yet no matter what happened, they'd always had each other. In fact, for years he'd hero-worshipped his older brother. Ryne had often picked up on the mood in the house and found them a place to hide until the storm that was his father passed out.

Well, those days were well in the past. And so were the brotherly feelings apparently. How was Ryne spending the night? Was he equally torn over the coming event?

He rolled over and punched his pillow into a more comfortable shape then settled his head on the cool surface. It did little to quiet his thoughts though, questions keeping sleep at bay. How long had Ryne been planning to issue a challenge? Was that why he'd been so moody all week? Or was it one of those rash decisions Ryne was known for?

Knowing he wouldn't get any rest, he got up and pulled on a pair of jeans before padding downstairs. The house was silent, the floor boards creaking faintly as he walked the familiar pathway. He intended to go for a run but a light shining at the end of the hall drew his attention. He hesitated, not really wanting to talk to anyone, but a sense of duty had him veering from his chosen path towards the kitchen. As he'd suspected, a lone figure was sitting at the table, a cup of tea in her hand.

"Hello, Kane." Helen addressed him without turning around.

"You're up late." He entered the room and pulled out a chair to sit in, the scraping of the legs on the floor sounding louder than normal in the silence of the night.

"I could say the same about you."

He shrugged. "I couldn't sleep."

"Me either." She stood and went to the cupboard and took out a cup. "I've been thinking about what you said. That someone tampered with Zack's brakes. I still can't believe anyone would do such a thing."

"I know. I was shocked when Ryne showed me the evidence."

"And you're sure it wasn't just an accident?" She poured water from the simmering kettle into a teapot and carried it to the table.

"Ryne's good with mechanics. He said it wasn't natural wear and tear. Especially not on a new truck."

"It was hard enough losing Zack, but this news…" Her voice trailed off and she sat down heavily. "It's been a hard day."

"Yes, it has." He scrubbed his face, then dragged his fingers back through his hair.

"The meeting tonight was quite a shock."

"To put it mildly."

She poured some tea into a cup and pushed it towards him. "Try this. It's camomile."

He looked at it skeptically. "I doubt a cup of tea will help."

"Nadia highly recommends it."

Nadia was their nurse practitioner, a font of modern scientific wisdom and medical folklore. He took a sip and made a face at the sweet flowery taste.

"The challenge is weighing on your mind." Helen prodded gently.

"Yeah." He stared down at the cup he now cradled in his hands. "Did I do the right thing, accepting the challenge? If I'd stepped down—"

"Ryne would be Alpha." Helen cocked her head. "Is that best for the pack?"

"Maybe… I don't know." He shrugged one shoulder.

"Will you be good for the pack?"

"Yes!" He looked up. "Of course."

"And that's why you made the choice you did. You want what's best for the pack."

He gave a short laugh. "Or maybe I have an over-inflated opinion of myself."

"Not you." Helen smiled. "Or at least not yet."

"Not yet?" He quirked a brow.

"I've seen a lot of Alphas in my time and some of them were pretty arrogant. Having a pack hanging onto your every word, almost worshipping the ground you walk on, can go to your head."

"I'll try to remember that."

"If you forget, I'll pull out my wooden spoon."

They both chuckled before the gravity of the situation once again invaded their thoughts.

"What the hell was Ryne thinking, Helen? He knows a challenge is to the death."

She nodded and blinked, a tear slowly dripping down her face. "You're both like my sons. I don't want either of you harmed. After losing Zack, I don't think I can handle much more."

"I know." He turned the cup in his hands thinking of all the times he, Ryne and Helen had sat at this very table having a late night conversation. She used to wait up for them when they were teens, claiming she couldn't sleep until she knew her boys were safely home. "I don't know if I can do this. He's my brother, Helen." He glanced up at her, not trying to hide the torment that twisted his gut.

"Kane, you know the Book of the Law better than most. Are you sure there isn't a way around this? Some sub-clause that could be used? A new interpretation that hasn't been considered before?" Helen reached out and touched his arm. "I remember when you and Ryne were at the Academy and studying for finals. There was a passage in one of your text books that you were debating."

He frowned as he searched his memory. "I remember that. The point was that the Book of the Law was written centuries ago. Alphas need to consider the spirit and intent of a law, rather than the exact wording, before enacting it."

"Maybe you can use that to your advantage?"

He leaned back in his chair, eyes narrowed and then slowly nodded. "Perhaps... Of course, it's a moot point unless I win."

"You will. I have faith in you."

He spent the rest of the night reading passages from the Book of the Law, checking precedents and considering his options. When he was done, it was almost morning. His eyes were gritty, his body weary and he hoped he hadn't made a mistake putting energy into planning his strategy rather than resting. Would he have enough strength now to defeat Ryne? He wasn't sure.

When light began to break, he headed out, shifting into wolf form to go for a slow run, not enough to tire himself, just to warm up and, of course, to see his territory one more time. Technically, it wasn't officially his, but he'd felt a deep connection to it ever since the day Helen and Zack had announced he and Ryne would, from then on, forever be part of their family.

He recalled the day the direction of his life had turned around. The previous night, his father had announced their family was leaving and he and Ryne had been silently packing their meagre possessions into bags. Every time they returned to Oregon, he'd hope their mother was telling the truth when she said they were there to stay. His father always ruined it though, causing trouble until the Alpha kicked them out. It happened no matter where they went until it reached the point he didn't dare make friends or get close to anyone because it never lasted. Leaving hurt too much if you became attached.

~~~

His mother entered the room, her face bearing signs of strain like always, lines around her mouth, shadows under her eyes. He'd seen pictures of her when she was younger; she'd been beautiful back then. Now, even to his young eyes, she looked older than her years.

"You can stop packing." She nodded towards the duffles.

"The bastard has changed his mind?" Ryne looked up, a t-shirt balled in his hand.

"Don't call him that. You need to show some respect to your father." She shot a sharp look at her eldest son.

Ryne snorted. "I only respect people who deserve it. Besides, he's not my father."

Trying to calm the situation, Kane spoke up. "The Alpha changed his mind and said we can stay?" He'd heard the argument the previous night; Alpha William and his father had waged a war of words outside his bedroom window.

"No, Kane." She shook her head. "We're leaving."

His stomach suddenly felt like it had ice in it. "So we can't take our stuff?" He didn't have much. A new shirt Helen had given him for his birthday. A battered copy of the Book of the Law Zack had shared when he'd expressed interest in learning more about pack law. Zack was the Beta and had always taken extra time with him, answering his questions.

"I mean, Carter and I are leaving. You're staying."

"We are?" He and Ryne spoke together.

"It's for the best." She pursed her lips. "Money is tight right now. You two are growing out of your clothes every day, eating like bottomless pits."

Ryne sneered. "Carter doesn't want to have to waste money on us."

"That's not the reason." She rubbed her arm.

Kane noticed the bruise marks on her arm. They were shaped like his father's hand. His own fingers curled into fists wishing he was big enough to defend her.

His mother continued speaking. "The Alpha feels it would be better if you had a stable home for a while. Carter is talking about heading south of the border and who knows what the schools will be like."

"So we get to stay here...for how long?" He ignored Ryne's mumbling that school had never figured in any of their moves before.

"I don't know." She reached out and ruffled his hair. "You're almost grown. It's not like you need your parents that much anymore."

He wasn't sure how he felt about that. Now eleven, almost twelve, there were days he felt like he was grown up. At other times, he really wished he had a mother who baked cookies like Helen and fussed over him when he was sick. And a father who paid attention like Zack and taught important things like tracking and reading the weather.

"Where will we live?" Ryne had folded his arms, eyes narrowed.

"Zack and Helen have agreed to take you in."

His eyes widened at the news and Ryne nodded in approval.

She looked at both of them and gave a tentative smile that didn't match the sheen of tears in her eyes. "I know you'll be happier here."

"Mom, I..." Kane shifted on his feet unsure what to say. She was his mother and he loved her in spite of everything. "Why don't you stay with us? You'd be safe here and—"

"No." She didn't let him finish. "Carter is my mate and mates stick together."

"Like you stayed with my father?" Ryne pointed out.

"That was...different. Things didn't work out. He...he didn't want to be mated to a female."

"What?" He cocked his head. "I don't understand."

"Never mind. It's not important." She shook her head. "The point is I'm going with Carter. He'll take care of me. Besides, he needs me. You know how he gets sometimes."

Yes, he knew. She loved them, but she didn't love them enough to leave his father. Damned bastard.

She took a deep breath. "I have to go now. Be good." She gave Ryne a quick hug and him as well, pressing a kiss to his forehead. "I'll keep in touch." With one final glance, she turned quickly and left.

He looked at Ryne, feeling a strange lump in his throat. "So, this is home now." He said the words tentatively, not certain if he should believe them and not even sure if he should be happy or sad.

Ryne looked around and nodded. "Yep." He picked up his duffle and dumped the contents on the bed. "I guess we're finally home."

"At least until they kick us out." He thought of all the times he'd believed he finally had a home only to have it all fall apart.

"Yeah." A hint of fear flickered over Ryne's face before it was hidden by the blank mask he wore so often.

Kane wet his lips and glanced towards the door. "Should we have asked to go with her anyway?"

"Nope." Ryne wandered over to where he stood and slung an arm around his shoulders. He seemed to be forcing a confident tone into his voice. "She's made her choice. And she's right. This is a good place for us. Don't worry, I'll take care of you."

"You're only thirteen," he scoffed.

"Old enough." And with that Ryne had flipped him over for a wrestling match…

~~~

The memory faded and he blinked. Looking around, he was surprised at how far he'd travelled. There was a large ravine nearby and he trotted to the edge. The air was cool, the rising sun only now starting to penetrate the shadows cast by the trees. Sitting down, eyes half-closed, he absorbed the scents and sights and sounds of the territory. They nourished his soul, filling him with contentment.

He loved this land and all who lived here and he'd do anything for them; Zack and Helen and the whole pack. They'd become the extended family he'd always longed for. If they hadn't taken him in, who knows how his life might have turned out.

About a year after moving in with Zack and Helen, the Alpha had stepped down and Zack had ascended to the position, the pack voting for him over the other contender, Dietrich. As Alpha, Zach had arranged for his foster sons to go to the Academy for training when they were old enough. Then, after graduation, he'd eventually given them both positions as Betas. It was more than either of them would ever have been able to achieve if they'd stayed with their parents. Yes, he owed a lot to this pack.

A sound drew his attention and he turned towards it. On the other side of the rugged ravine stood a black wolf. It was glaring at him, head lowered, a low rumble emitting from its throat and travelling across the divide towards him

It was Ryne, the brother who'd promised to always take care of him.

Chapter 5

The appointed time of the challenge fight arrived. Kane stood on one side of the small clearing, Ryne on the other. A neutral observer from OPATA, the Office of Pack Administration and Territory Allotment, a division of Lycan Link, stood in the middle. He didn't look pleased. No doubt his weekend plans had been ruined by the emergency call the Council of Elders had placed. The man flicked a look at those gathered, rattled the paper in hand authoritatively and cleared his throat before reading the rules to those gathered.

"Opponents step forward." The man pointed to spots on either side of himself, approximately six feet apart.

The brothers approached, eyes meeting and then looking away. Ryne was edgy, bouncing on his toes, his hands clenching and unclenching, jaw tight. Kane exhaled slowly, keeping his wolf under control, not wasting energy on nervous movement.

"The first ten minutes will be fought in human form. Should the fight continue beyond that point, I'll give the signal and you may shift into wolves." The official glanced at both of them and they nodded.

It was standard procedure. Since the human half of a Lycan was considered the dominant member, they needed to prove their worth first. If the combatants made it beyond ten minutes then they were likely equally matched and the wolves would then be tested.

The official continued to outline the rules. "The fight will continue until there is a victor or one of the combatants admits defeat or revokes the challenge. If I see evidence of foul play, I will call a halt and both of you will stand down. Foul play includes the use of weapons or interference from other Lycans or outside forces. This includes magic if any such beings are present." He scanned the crowd before continuing. "As the designated spokesperson, I must state on OPATA's behalf that, in principle, they disapprove of a challenge to the death. Having said that, they also acknowledge that it is allowed under the Book of the Law. Do you understand and agree with the terms?"

"Yes." Ryne spoke first.

Kane nodded, swallowed and then answered. "I do."

The official stepped back several paces and then nodded. "Begin."

In a flash, Ryne moved, striking hard and sending Kane reeling backward to the ground. Fists swinging, he began to pummel his opponent until Kane managed to flip them over, striking blows of his own. They fought for dominance, frequently changing position, the advantage see-sawing back and forth.

Kane pulled back and sprang to his feet, Ryne following suit only to stumble as Kane kicked out, knocking him down. Ryne reached out grabbing Kane's ankle, pulling him off balance so they were once more tumbling in the dirt. Grunts, panting, curses and soft cries of pain filled the air.

"You deceiving bastard." Ryne's fist plowed into Kane's mouth. "Zack trusted you."

"What the hell are you talking about?" Kane spat out blood as he dodged another punch while delivering one of his own.

"You know damned well." Ryne panted. "The truck. You had it all planned."

"What about the fucking truck?" Kane barely had time to clench his stomach muscles before Ryne slammed his knee into his gut.

"You took it for a drive. You admitted it."

"So?" He dodged a blow that was aimed at his chin.

"Don't play the innocent with me." Ryne wrapped his fingers around Kane's throat. "I'll never grovel before the likes of you."

Kane wheezed, his hands on Ryne's as he tried to pry away the fingers that were squeezing his windpipe. His arms trembled with the effort and then he was free, sucking in mouthfuls of air before launching his own attack.

They rolled over and over, equally matched, the balance of power shifting every few seconds. Part of Kane's brain noted the smell of alcohol on Ryne and he wondered at the man's stupidity. Even a fool knew keeping your wits about you was key to a fight.

A whistle pierced the air followed by the official's voice. "Time. Opponents shift forms."

The air shimmered and two black wolves appeared. Snarling, they attacked using tooth and claw against each other. Ryne fought like a demon, some inner rage driving him into a frenzy of activity. Clouds of dust rose around them as they tumbled about, claws digging into the ground for traction, growls and the scent of blood filling the air.

Kane tried to hold back, letting his brother expend his energy. He retreated to minimize injury while waiting for the right moment to strike. Cool logic was his plan, knowing Ryne couldn't keep up his frenzied assault for too long.

His strategy slowly began to work. Ryne was tiring, his breathing laboured. Kane shook his head to clear the blood from his eyes. He knew he was injured but ignored the pain. Now was the time to act. Digging deep, he began to deliver his offensive attacks, darting in and out, nipping at legs, going for the hamstring, the belly.

Ryne twisted and turned, trying to avoid him and that was when Kane saw his opening. He slammed into Ryne knocking him down and grabbing him by the throat. Ryne's hind legs scrambled wildly, catching Kane in the belly but he didn't let go despite the feel of his flesh tearing. He bit down harder, cutting off Ryne's air until he felt him go limp.

Only then did he step back, exhausted and panting, hoping he'd only subdued his brother and not killed him. He shifted back to human form using his own energy to force Ryne to change as well.

"Get up!" He growled the words, chest heaving as he struggled to catch his breath. Sweat dripped down his face as he narrowed his eyes keeping them fixed at the man at his feet.

Ryne stared up at him with obvious hatred yet made no effort to move. His lip was split, one eye almost swollen shut. Various bruises and scratches adorned the rest of him, blood dripping from the numerous gashes.

Kane knew he must look the same. He could feel blood streaming from his side, soaking what remained of his clothing. Truth be told, he was feeling the effects of blood-loss, the edges of his vision starting to darken. He hid it though, no sign of weakness showing outwardly. This was a battle for leadership of the pack and ancient instincts wouldn't allow him to concede defeat.

Ryne continued to glare at him from the ground. The last blow had robbed the man of his breath, giving Kane a momentary advantage. Now the question was whether Ryne would resume the fight or not. If he did, it would be to the death; they'd gone beyond the point of any other option.

"Get up and fight…brother!" He spat out the last word while praying Ryne would concede. His hours pouring over the Book of the Law had given him a loop hole, provided he had a chance to use it. The law stated the victor of a challenge became Alpha, it didn't specifically say the other challenger had to die. Rather, it said all who lived in the pack would bow before him and be subject to his decrees. His dictates would be abided by the members, upon the fear of death.

The death, or life, of any pack member had always been in the hands of the Alpha. In ancient times, the victor would often choose to kill their opponent, but he'd argue they'd evolved beyond that point, that killing to maintain power was turning their backs on all the advances made and to once again become little more than creatures governed solely by ancient instincts.

So that was his plan…if the cards fell in his favour.

Seconds ticked by, the gathered crowd silently awaiting the outcome that would decide the future Alpha of the pack. Kane was prepared for another attack, knowing Ryne was weighing his options. The animal within Kane was thirsting for blood but, as always, he was in control. That was his advantage. He acted with cool logic whereas Ryne was the impulsive hothead.

There was a flicker in Ryne's eyes and then he slowly shifted his eyes to the side and down. A small gesture but significant. The battle was over.

"Kane is the winner of the challenge." With a nod, the OPATA observer declared the outcome.

Those assembled murmured at the news. There was no cry of victory nor sounds of discontent. Both men had their share of supporters, both had qualities that would make them good leaders but the pack accepted the results unilaterally. It was the way of their people.

"I am Alpha."

Kane made the statement loudly, widening his stance, hands on his hips as he met the gazes of the Lycans gathered, mostly members of the Council of Elders and few other higher ranking Lycans. No Marla; a corner of his mind acknowledged the fact before returning to establishing his dominance. Each person present lowered their eyes, showing their submission. No one challenged him. A feeling of pride swelled within him, the power and elation that came with victory.

"As for my opponent, Ryne Taylor. I will allow him to live."

The crowd gasped but he paid them no mind.

"I will allow him to live, not out of brotherly love—there is little of that left between us—but because the needs of this pack are foremost in my mind. Ryne has many friends within our pack and his death would serve no purpose except to cause grief, division, and discord at a time when we need to be unified."

He turned to face Ryne, hand extended. The heat of battle, the need to be dominant would leave them now and hopefully they could repair their relationship. They'd been co-Betas and after a cooling off period, he'd offer Ryne the Beta position again except...Ryne was no longer there.

"Ryne?" He called out the man's name, turning in a circle, peering into the trees that surrounded the clearing where the fight took place.

"He's gone, Alpha." John stepped forward. "He slunk away as soon as you said he would live."

He nodded slowly, hoping Ryne would be all right. They might have been opponents but the man was still his brother. He kept his thoughts to himself, however. Strength and decisiveness were needed now as he established his control. "John, I'm appointing you as my Beta, if that's agreeable with you."

John nodded. "Thank you. I'll do my best to serve you."

"Excellent." He clapped his hand on the man's shoulder. "Your first duty is to take me to the medical centre. I think Nadia needs to put a stitch or two into me."

John glanced at the blood-soaked clothing and nodded. "I'd say that's a good decision." He jerked his chin towards the others gathered. "What about them?"

Kane looked at his pack members. "Spread the news of the results and that I'll address the pack tonight at seven."

He walked to the car and, tossing the keys to John, slid into the passenger seat.

"Being Beta means I'm your chauffeur?" John gave him a teasing glance.

"Yeah. Home James, or whatever it is the rich and famous say." He leaned his head back, coughing, struggling to breathe. Now that he didn't need to put on a show of strength for the pack, he was starting to feel like he'd pass out. "Except, make that the infirmary."

Chapter 6

Hours later, Kane stood beside the podium facing the members of his pack. In some ways it was surreal, the events of the past week like a blur. He'd never imagined himself in this position at such a young age. Someday, but not now. In other ways, it was all too real. The expectant faces before him, the gauze on his side protecting his stitches.

Nadia, their nurse practitioner, had nearly had a fit when John had dragged him into the infirmary. His knees had kept giving out on him as he swam in and out of consciousness.

~~~

"What the hell happened to you? I go away for a few days and this is what you get up to?" She cut off the remains of his bloody shirt as he lay on the gurney, fighting to draw air into his lungs.

"I'm the new Alpha." He gave a crooked grin as he struggled to form the words.

"More like the half-dead Alpha." She hissed as she saw the wound. "Damned fools. Where is your opponent? Already in the grave?"

He shook his head. "No idea. He left."

"I saw him leave," John added. "He was limping but looked better than our new Alpha here."

Kane gave a sigh of relief. He'd been worried. His goal had been to win the fight while causing the minimum amount of damage. Seems like he must have been successful.

"Ouch!" He winced as Nadia probed his wound. Too bad Ryne hadn't been following the same principles.

"Well, if he shows up here, I'll treat him as well. Medicine doesn't discriminate against stupidity." Nadia scowled, mumbling to herself as she enumerated the injuries. "Laceration to the side, approximately two inches deep, a probable pneumothorax—"

"Is that bad?" John asked.

"Well it sure as hell isn't a walk in the park picking daisies! Don't ask idiotic questions," Nadia pushed John aside and wheeled an oxygen tank over to where Kane was and then made her way to the cabinet that contained some of her medical supplies. "Kane, I'll give you some oxygen to help you breathe while I prep for surgery."

"Surgery?" He coughed as he tried to sit up. "I have to address the pack tonight."

She pressed him back down and fit a clear plastic tube for oxygen over his face. "And you need to be alive and breathing to do it. Now stay put or I'll give you a sedative that will knock you out for a week!"

There was a glint in her eye that had him subsiding. "What kind of surgery?" His voice sounded stronger, the oxygen from the nasal cannula making it easier to breathe and talk.

"I'll know better once I get x-rays of your lungs and I can examine the wound better. Right now, I suspect I'll need to insert a chest tube to get rid of the air that's accumulated between the inside of the chest and the outside of the lung. Stitches to close the gash in your side. And I'm hoping nothing else was nicked or I'll be patching up your insides as well."

She continued to mutter and berate him right up to the time she knocked him out.

~~~

It had been a battle to get her to disconnect his IV so he could attend this meeting. He looked to where she was now standing, watching him like a hawk. As soon as he was done here, she wanted him back at the infirmary. Truth be told, he wished he was there now. He felt as weak as a newborn pup. With any luck, this would go down as the shortest pack meeting in history and he'd be able to get his ass back into bed.

He shifted his weight and barely managed to hold back a wince as pain shot from his side. Another glance at Nadia revealed she was giving him a look that screamed 'I told you so'. The corner of his mouth twitched. Her acerbic attitude was entertaining...in small doses. On a permanent basis, he'd prefer a sweet, gentle woman.

Like the girl at the movies? His inner wolf queried.

Perhaps. If we ever met again, she might prove to match the mental fantasy that had developed around her.

The wolf thumped its tail in approval and then subsided. It too was worn out from the fight earlier in the day.

Kane left off his mental musings when the sound of the gavel banging drew his attention. William was calling the meeting to order. The older man had been Alpha before Zack and was viewed by many in a grandfatherly light.

"Members of the pack, as you know a challenge was issued for the position of Alpha. Under the supervision of OPATA, the fight occurred just before noon and Kane Sinclair emerged victorious. I bow before you, Alpha Kane."

The membership stood and as one followed suit. "We bow before you, Alpha."

Kane nodded and William stepped to the side as he took his place behind the podium. An odd thrill washed over him. It would now be his spot at every meeting until his death or he abdicated.

"I am Alpha." He spoke the phrase loudly, using the same power and conviction of all the Alphas who had held the position before him. There could be no doubt in his voice, no wavering in his gaze as he swept it over those assembled before him. "I will serve you, guide you and guard you with my life."

The pack responded in the age-old tradition. "We will follow your dictates, respect your wisdom, serve you and guard you with our lives."

William stepped forward again. "As Kane is already a member of our pack, there is no need for a symbolic mixing of our blood." He scanned the room but no one protested.

Out of the corner of his eye, Kane saw Nadia making a face likely thinking he'd already shed enough blood that day. The corner of his mouth twitched again. She came across as hard-nosed but he knew she had a quirky sense of humour that few realized.

"Kane," William spoke his name. "Please sign your name in the front of the Book of the Law."

Kane stepped over to the table and watched as William took the ancient tome from its place on the shelf. The book was centuries old, dating back to the time the pack was first formed. The front pages listed all the Alphas that had served before him; Caius,

Gregor, Primus, Theo… He wasn't ashamed that his hand trembled slightly as he picked up the pen and added his name to the list. It was now his duty to ensure the pack continued to grow and thrive. His decisions and actions would impact future generations. He swallowed hard hoping in centuries to come his years of rule would be looked upon favourably.

William witnessed his signature. "It is done."

Everyone applauded and Kane returned to the podium to address his pack. *His pack.* The phrase made his heart swell.

"I thank you for your welcome and know I can count on you for your support. I'm sure many of you have questions, perhaps personal concerns you'd like to bring to my attention. Rest assured, I will try to be available to all of you. Unfortunately, a pressing matter prevents me from having a Q&A right now."

"Is this to do with Ryne?" Someone shouted from the back. "You didn't kill him as protocol dictates."

He tightened his lips. It was an issue he planned to address, just not today. The heckler, however, was testing his authority and a response was needed. "Step forward and address me properly." He growled the words letting all present know he was displeased.

A young man walked to the front of the room and stopped a few yards from the podium. He was barely beyond a pup. His face pale, he kept glancing behind him. No doubt he'd been dared by his friends.

"You're Joshua, correct?"

"Yes, Alpha." The boy nodded and swallowed hard.

"What did I say before you shouted out your question?" Folding his arms, Kane rested them on the podium and arched one brow.

"That...that you had pressing matters to deal with." Joshua's voice cracked mid-sentence.

"I'm pleased to know your hearing isn't faulty." He raised his eyes to the membership knowing they were wondering if he'd answer the boy's initial question. To do so would be a sign of weakness, a contradiction of his statement that questions would be answered another day. He'd not be tricked in such an amateurish manner. "The meeting is concluded. Questions will be answered as soon as my schedule allows. You are all dismissed."

He pushed off from the podium and began to walk to the door where Nadia was tapping her foot. Neither his posture nor stride showed he was feeling weak or in pain. As he passed the young man who seemed frozen in place, he gave him a nod. "Have a good evening, Joshua. And remember, friends who dare you to do something stupid aren't the friends you need."

"I will Alpha. Thank you, Alpha."

Somehow, he managed to avoid being detained by anyone and slid gratefully into Nadia's car. A sigh escaped him as he relaxed into the cushioned surface. "I'm exhausted, just like you predicted."

She didn't say anything, merely raising a brow and starting the car. It was a short drive to the infirmary, completed in silence. He didn't mind, being too tired to talk. Once they reached their destination. Nadia ushered him inside.

"Shirt off."

He bit back a groan as he removed his shirt, the movement of his arm pulling on the wound. Throwing the garment on a nearby chair, he sat on the side of the bed.

Nadia checked his bandages, her hands steady and professional as they skimmed over him. "No bleeding. Good."

"I tried not to move too much." He toed off his shoes, eager to lie down and rest.

"You handled the meeting well."

"Thanks."

"I heard what you said to Joshua. Good advice." She handed him two pain pills and then a glass of water. "Take these."

His side was throbbing enough he didn't even quibble over taking the medication. "He's a good kid. He just needs to learn to think for himself."

"It can be hard to balance; pack mentality is important—"

"To a certain extent." He leaned back, sighing as his head touched the cool pillow. "Blindly following a stupid idea is just—"

"Stupid?"

"Yeah." He laughed and then winced.

She smiled. "Goodnight...Alpha."

Chapter 7

The following weeks were a whirlwind of activity. Kane had meetings with the pack lawyer and accountant to go over pack finances and investments as well as completing the mandatory forms to ensure his name was on all official documents for Lycan Link. The question and answer session he'd promised the pack happened and he did his best to ease any fears the members might have had over the transition of power.

Surprisingly enough, it was Helen who had a concern, though she expressed it privately.

"I'll be packing my things this weekend." She made the announcement over breakfast one morning.

"What?" He nearly choked on his coffee. "Why?"

"You're Alpha now. This is your house. You and your mate will need the room." She made the statement in a matter of fact manner, punctuating it by cracking an egg into the frying pan.

"Wait a minute. What mate? And this is your home, Helen. I'm not kicking you out."

"You're a young, handsome and unmarried Alpha. You'll have a mate soon." She nodded as she dropped the egg shells into the compost container. "Besides, that suite of rooms upstairs is too big for me."

"Helen, you can't leave. I need you."

"Why?"

"Well..." His stomach chose to growl at that moment and he took it as a sign. "Who will cook for me?"

She laughed. "You know darned well how to cook. I taught you, so don't try to pull that one on me."

"Sorry. That was a dumb reason. But..." He tried to think of another argument for her to stay. "I'll still need a hostess for a while. I've no intention of finding a mate anytime soon."

"John's Carrie will help out."

"She's going to be busy with a new pup." He stood up and walked over to where Helen stood, turning her to face him and then crouching down a bit so they were eye to eye. "This is your home. There's no need to leave. If and when I ever find a mate, she'll be busy raising our pups and helping me."

"Well..." Helen looked away.

He could sense her indecision, knew in his gut that she didn't really want to go and was probably offering to leave out of some misplaced sense of propriety. He pressed his point.

"When you and Zack took over, the girls, Ryne and I were already teenagers. Can you imagine how busy you would have been raising pups and being female Alpha all by yourself?"

She considered his words. "It is a busy time... But that suite of rooms holds too many memories."

"Then switch rooms. There's a housekeeper's unit that hasn't been used in ages. You could move in there."

"I don't know..."

"Listen, you've taken the place of my mother for years. Hell, you've been *more* of a mother to me than she ever was. I can't kick you out of the house!"

"Mother? Oh Kane!" Her eyes got misty and she reached out to squeeze his hand.

"You can stay here and be a...a den mother!" He grinned, pleased with his idea.

"I..." She looked about the kitchen. "I would miss this place and I really don't know what I'll do with my time."

"Well, I'm sure your girls would love to have your help, but I need you more. I'm a poor bachelor after all." He tried to look helpless.

"Ha!"

He laughed and then rubbed his hands together. "Then it's decided. I'll get someone here today and you tell him if you want any changes to the housekeeper's unit. And I'll inform the Council of your new official title when we meet today."

"And you can take over my suite of rooms. Maybe even put a doorway between your current room and the one Zack and I used. The whole wing of the house could be yours then."

"I don't need that much space."

"You will." She gave him a knowing look. "Once you start a family, you'll be glad to have those rooms."

He rolled his eyes. Settling down wasn't on his list quite yet. Getting settled into his role as Alpha would consume most of his time and energy for the foreseeable future. Starting a family wasn't even on the horizon.

His meeting with the Elders didn't go quite as planned. Oh, they'd been pleased with Helen's new role, however there were more pressing matters on their mind.

"Ryne is out to sabotage the pack." William announced.

"How so?" Kane folded his hands on the table, trying to keep them from tensing. Many of the pack had it in for Ryne, while he...he still felt a fraternal connection that was hard to deny. Yes, they'd fought but he hoped for a reconciliation at some future date.

"Since Zack's accident, a lot of things have gone wrong around here. Our electricity was turned off for non-payment two weeks ago, even though the bill had been paid," one Elder said.

"And last week the Fire Marshall was here, wanting to inspect all the buildings because of an anonymous tip," another Elder pointed out.

William nodded. "We've had traps set on the property and hunters spotted on our land."

Kane shrugged. "Hunters are always a problem."

"True," William agreed. "But a scout reported an oil slick near the mouth of the river yesterday. It's killed off some of the wildlife."

He felt himself pale at the news even as anger coursed through him. Surging to his feet, the sound of his chair being roughly shoved back punctuated his movement. Hands curled at his sides, he glared at the group. "Why wasn't I told of this?"

"We're telling you now."

"I am the Alpha of this pack." He pointed to his chest. "The scouts should be reporting to me or at the very least, John." He swept his eyes over the group. "How long has this been going on?"

"You were ill the first week, Kane." One of them began to explain. "We felt it best—"

"No." He brought his fist down on the table. "I'll not be finding out news second-hand. The Council of Elders is here to advise me, not to filter the information I do or do not receive."

The group seemed taken aback but nodded.

"I'll check out the site of the spill this afternoon. As for Ryne being responsible, I'll assess the evidence myself before coming to any conclusions." He folded his arms. "You are dismissed."

He watched as they filed out. William hung back until the others were gone.

"Yes?" He arched a brow at the man.

"You did well, Kane."

"Pardon?"

"The Council of Elders contains many wise members but, like the rest of the pack, they will test your strength in various ways to ensure you are fit. You passed the first hurdle." William gave him a wink before leaving.

That was the first hurdle? He rubbed the back of his neck wondering what was next.

That afternoon, he headed out to where the oil spill had been found, hoping it wasn't too extensive. He had no experience with such an occurrence but the news reports of other spills he'd seen on TV led him to believe it wouldn't be an easy fix. He'd have to contact an environmentalist to assess the damage, buy some booms to help contain the oil, perhaps hire wildlife specialists to help rehabilitate any animals that had been affected.

It took some time to reach the location, an area where a highway crossed a corner of their property. The distance and rocky terrain meant it was seldom visited so who knew how long the oil had been there. As he surveyed the area, his brows lowered at the destruction before him.

An oil slick covered the water, the iridescent colours slowly spreading outward like a macabre rainbow, eddying around the dead fish that floated on the surface, their silvery white bellies starkly contrasting the evil darkness that killed all it touched. Along the shore, plants were already drooping from the poison while several dead animals and birds lay covered in the toxic sticky goo.

The sight sickened him, a muscle pulsed in his jaw as he took in the destruction. Where did he even start? Mid-thought, a slight movement caught his attention and he slid down the river bank to the location. It was a duckling struggling weakly to free itself. Nearby, its siblings were already dead.

He bent and picked it up, the tiny body seeming even more fragile in his much larger hand. With the tip of a finger, he tried to gently brush the oil from its bill and soft down. Dark button eyes blinked up at him, its fluttering heartbeat visible against its chest.

"Hey there, little guy. Don't worry." He kept his voice soft and hopefully soothing. "I'll take you back to the pack house and get you cleaned up."

Even as he spoke, the small creature trembled in his hand and then went completely limp, its head hanging lifelessly to the side.

He pressed his lips together. This small soul had been part of his territory and he'd been too late to save it. Rage filled him as he bent to set the dead animal on the ground, his inner wolf howling at the senseless waste of life.

Whoever did this had to pay!

A sound caught his attention and he turned, scanning the trees until he located a flash of blonde hair.

"Marla?" He called out her name.

"Kane?" She picked her way over to him, stepping over logs and ducking under low hanging branches. "I'm surprised to see you here."

"I could say the same thing."

She dropped her gaze. "I'm sorry. I...I'll leave. I know this is your territory."

"And yours."

"But..." She looked at him, her head tilted to the side, clearly puzzled. "Ryne lost and, naturally, I was on his side."

"This will always be your pack, Marla, as long as you want it to be." He folded his arms and quirked his brow. "I am surprised you aren't with Ryne though."

"Oh." She looked away. "When he lost, he said he was going to leave the area. I was going to go with him but he's been acting differently lately. I...I'm sort of scared of him."

"Scared?"

She twisted her fingers. "Ryne's been talking crazy, more quick-tempered than usual. I..." She paused and took a deep breath. "I broke up with him, said I didn't want to leave. He stormed out and I haven't seen him since."

He nodded. Yeah, Ryne wouldn't take that well. After losing the challenge, having his girlfriend dump him would really tip the balance.

"This is a mess." Marla looked at the oily mess and wrinkled her nose.

"We just discovered it. I've no idea how long it's been here since no one hardly ever visits this area." He frowned. "Which makes me wonder why you're here. You're not a nature lover."

"Well," she began slowly, seeming to consider her words carefully. "As I said, I broke up with Ryne and he left but I think he's still in the area. I was going to try to talk to him, get him to try and patch things up with you. I know how close you were and this rift must be so hard for you." She reached out and touched his hand gently.

He nodded, acknowledging her gesture despite the fact his wolf was muttering darkly. The animal had been more on edge since becoming Alpha. It would take it time to settle into the new role. And it probably associated Marla with Ryne. His wolf wasn't quick to forgive. They'd have to have a long talk about that once there was some spare time.

She shrugged. "Anyway, I was following his scent along the highway when it veered from the road and came this way."

"Thanks for the information, but you shouldn't be here. Who knows how toxic this area is? I'll see if I can pick up Ryne's trail once we get you back to safety." He began to lead her away.

"You're so good to me." She clasped his arm. "You're going to make a wonderful Alpha."

"Going to?" He gave her a sideways look.

She laughed. "Sorry. We've been friends for so long, its hard to remember you *are* Alpha." The smile faded from her face. "The night Ryne issued the challenge I tried to talk him out of it." She shook her head. "You know what he can be like."

Yes, he knew Ryne very well...or at least he thought he did. He surveyed the oil slick one more time. Ryne could be impulsive but...was he also vindictive?

The rest of the week was spent getting the wheels in motion to deal with the oil spill. He issued his first edict as Alpha; no one was to use the water until they had a report back on its safety, and no one could go into the spill area without his express permission. Having no idea how far the contamination went or if it had leached into the water table their wells drew from, he'd rather err on the side of caution.

Being Alpha of such a large pack was a busier job than he'd realised. As Beta, he'd had some inkling but being the one responsible for all the decisions was tiring. It seemed he was always on call, everyone wanting a moment of his time.

He yawned and scrubbed his face, his elbows resting on the desk in his new office. It was Friday night and he was thinking fondly of evenings out with Ryne, visiting a local bar for a drink, a game of pool and perhaps a bit of companionship. There was no time for that now. And no brother to do it with.

A knock on the door had him sighing. "Yes?"

William and a few members of the Council of Elders entered.

"Kane, we thought we'd find you here." One nodded in approval.

"Paperwork." He gestured towards the stack of reports at his elbow. "What can I do for you?"

"It's actually what *we* can do for *you*."

A picture was handed to him and he glanced at it then did a double take. If he didn't know better, he'd swear it was the girl he'd seen at the movies, the one who invaded his thoughts at the oddest of times and soothed him to sleep late at night. But it couldn't be...could it? "Who is this?"

"She's yours." William announced.

"Mine?" He blinked wondering how the Council could know about his secret obsession. "What do you mean?"

"Most wolves, by the time they reach the status of Alpha, are mated. You're young, unattached and far too busy dealing with our large pack to find your own mate. She's suitable." The Elder speaking nodded as if it were a done deal.

"Now wait a minute." He pushed to his feet. "William, is this another of those hurdles you mentioned?"

"No, Kane. I'm afraid not." William sighed and shook his head. "Our pack is large, wealthy and powerful. You'll soon be a target for every pack that wants to make a favourable alliance. They'll find any excuse they can to parade their females in front of you."

"We're trying to be proactive," another explained. "You have no attachment to any of our own females. This girl is from the Rock Valley pack. As you know, it's of equal status to ours. Her father is the Alpha and agrees it would be a suitable match."

"I have no plans—"

"Think about it, Kane." William interrupted and patted him on the shoulder. "It would be good for you to have a mate and an alliance between our packs would make us a formidable force when it came to negotiations."

The others nodded. "We'll take you to meet her next week. No pressure. She won't even know why you're there."

He looked at the picture in his hands again. This turn of events completely blind-sided him and he couldn't even think of what to say. His silence must have been taken as agreement, for the Council left, looking quite pleased.

Once the room was empty, he dropped the picture onto his desk and began to pace. Yeah, just what every man wanted, someone picking out a mate for him. He'd find his own mate in his own time...if he ever had time. His eyes rested on the stack of paperwork just as his phone rang. With a sigh, he answered the call, listening politely as a pack member expressed concerns about some minor issue.

Half an hour later, he hung up and sat down to begin the paperwork he'd yet to complete.

The picture of the girl was sitting on his desk and he picked it up. She really was lovely and, if she was from the neighbouring pack, she could very well be the girl he'd seen at the theatre. He flipped the photo over.

Her name was on the back as well as a few other bits of information.

Elise Robinson. Eighteen years old. Youngest daughter of the Alpha.

He shook his head. She was still a teenager for heaven's sake. How could someone so young be the Alpha female? Setting the picture aside he tried to continue working except his eyes kept drifting back to the photo and her soft, gentle smile. There was a sweet innocence about her that drew him in.

We will teach her, protect her, his wolf whispered.

No, it was utter nonsense. Arranged marriages were archaic. The girl was probably mortified at the very idea.

Chapter 8

"What do you mean, she doesn't know?" Kane ran his hands through his hair, not pleased with what he'd just learned.

It was exactly one week after the Council had presented him with the idea of taking a mate. His own secret obsession with the girl and his wolf's prodding had made him agree to a meeting while not committing to anything. Now he stood in Alpha Robinson's office and, after an hour of negotiations, he'd just discovered this girl, Elise, had no idea of what was in the works.

"There's no point in getting her hopes up if we decide the alliance isn't favourable, is there?" One of the Elders explained.

He scowled, not liking the air of subterfuge.

"Elise is young. Her head's in the clouds." Her father waved his hand negligently. "Being an Alpha's mate is every young girl's dream."

Kane eyed the man. He seemed old to have a daughter so young, his hair liberally sprinkled with grey, lines around his eyes and mouth. There was a hard air about the man, as if he'd closed himself off to all feeling. Did he have the slightest idea as to what his daughter really wanted?

"I'd still like to meet her." Kane pressed his point.

"You've seen her picture. She's pretty and usually quite biddable. She'll bear you fine pups." The

Alpha rose from his seat and moved to a set of French doors, pulling the curtains aside.

Once again Kane felt himself frowning, feeling this was more like negotiations to buy a brood mare.

"If you insist on seeing her, look out the window. She's in the backyard right now warming up before her daily run."

He walked to the window to look out, scanning the area until he caught sight of someone near the edge of the woods. His inner wolf perked its ears. It was definitely the girl from the theatre!

She was average height with long slim legs and gentle curves. Her dark brown hair was pulled back in a pony tail and he caught glimpses of her smile and bright green eyes as she turned to talk to someone. Drawn by some inner need, he cracked open the door and inhaled, sorting through the scents until he caught hers. Yes! Exactly as he remembered. It seemed to curl around him, filling him with desire. His wolf growled in approval...until a male appeared and stood beside the girl.

"Who is that with her?" He spoke over his shoulder not taking his eyes off her, resisting the urge to stalk over to where they stood and shove the man away.

"Bryan Cooper, one of her friends. Don't worry, he's of no consequence. I've given him a stern warning not to touch her. I can guarantee she's a virgin."

"We'd want proof, of course." One of the Elders spoke behind him but Kane didn't turn. His eyes were fixed on Elise, watching her move, hearing the sound of her laughter floating on the breeze. He paid little attention to the rest of the meeting, both he and his wolf focused on the female. It wouldn't be a hardship to be mated to her. As an Alpha's daughter, she'd understand his time would be occupied with pack business. Perhaps this would work. He'd insist she be told though, an unwilling mate didn't appeal to him at all.

"Kane, I just heard the news!"

He looked up, his coffee cup half raised to his mouth, as Marla entered the kitchen of the pack house. "What news is that?"

"That you might be mated with some little girl from another pack in order to form an alliance. The entire pack is abuzz about it."

He nodded. "I'm seriously considering it for the good of the pack. Our land borders theirs. It will ensure stability and peaceful relations plus we'll be able to work together to keep out human developers and companies like Northern Oil." His own attraction to Elise was an added bonus he didn't feel needed to be mentioned.

"Kane, you're an amazing Alpha and this is very noble of you, but no one would want you to sacrifice your personal happiness."

He smiled appreciating her concern.

Marla had taken to spending more time here now that Ryne was gone...or supposedly gone. He'd followed the scent trail she'd told him about and it did seem his brother had been in the area. Ryne's scent had also turned up in other areas as well, near leg traps, along pathways. His lips tightened as he wondered what the hell his brother was up to. Sabotaging the pack made no sense. Marla's explanation was that Ryne was unhinged. Perhaps she knew what she was talking about. She'd been the closest to him for the past few months. He remembered Ryne's smug grin when he'd shared the news of the relationship. It seemed like only the other day ...

~~~

"Northern Oil sent us another request." Zack handed copies of the letter to both him and Ryne. They were having their weekly meeting, going over patrol schedules and discussing various issues that members had presented to them.

"We're not allowing them access to our land, are we?" Kane scanned the contents of the letter before giving Zack a questioning look.

"Hell no." Zack shook his head.

"Marla's been looking into the matter. She says it's a very reputable company," Ryne murmured as he read.

"Marla?" Zack arched a brow. "You've been spending a lot of time with her."

Ryne tossed the letter on the desk and grinned. "Yep."

"We might as well rent out your room," Kane teased his brother. "You never use it."

"Marla keeps me busy." Ryne leaned back in his chair. "I might make our relationship permanent."

"What?" He didn't even try to hide his surprise. He'd dated Marla himself a few times and knew the woman could be a handful. Truth be told, he felt responsible for her and often viewed himself in the role of big brother. When she'd moved on to Ryne, it had been strange to be relieved of the duty even though he'd tried to keep their relationship on a 'just friends' level. Marla had always been demanding of his time and attention, making their relationship out to be more than it was. It was her insecurity, of course, and he'd let it slide, ignoring the rumours they'd been deeply involved.

"Jealous, Bro?" Ryne gave him an assessing look.

"No." He replied flatly. "We had this conversation when you started dating her, remember?"

72

"Yeah, I said it was for your own good. She had you wrapped around her little finger."

"And I told you she's a friend and I feel a sense of responsibility towards her but that's it. You're welcome to her."

Zack interrupted. "Enough of the posturing. Ryne are you serious about this?"

"Marla and I are a good fit. She supports my photography, helps me arrange showings." He smirked and gave a wink. "Plus, there are other benefits, if you know what I mean."

Zack leaned forward, hands clasped on top of the desk. "Think this through, Ryne. Marla's a member of our pack but—"

"I know she can be difficult, but I can handle her. Besides, I like a challenge." Ryne rose to his feet. "And speaking of Marla, I promised to pick her up at work. Her shift at Bastian's is almost over."

~~~

"Kane?"

He blinked and realized Marla was speaking.

"Sorry, Marla, I was just thinking."

"I'm sure you were. You have a lot on your plate right now. And that's another reason you shouldn't rush into this arranged mating. The negotiations with Northern Oil—"

"The lawyers are dealing with that. Our position is 'no' regardless of what they offer."

"Oh." An odd expression flickered over her face before her features smoothed. "Well, then there's Ryne. I...I have some bad news."

"Bad news?"

"Well, maybe. I'm not sure." She paused, frowning. "I don't want to upset you..."

He barely kept from rolling his eyes, not in the mood for prevarication. "Marla, just tell me."

She took a deep breath and then began. "I was cleaning my apartment, going through the entryway closet and gathering up things Ryne had left behind. Shoved at the very back, I found bolt cutters and a shirt with some kind of goldish stain. I think it's brake fluid."

"Ryne often worked on his car. I don't—" He stopped, suddenly realizing the implications. "No. Ryne wouldn't do that."

Marla shrugged. "I'm not saying he's responsible for Zack's accident, but it does seem quite a coincidence."

"Yes. Yes, it is." His hand tightened on the cup cradled in his hand until it cracked, coffee spilling out over his fingers and onto the floor. "Damn!"

"Kane! Are you okay? Did you cut yourself?" Marla hurried after him as he made his way to the sink.

He set the cracked remains of the cup in the sink and checked his palm. A faint line of red showed where a shard had punctured the skin. He turned on the tap and ran water over the injury. "I'm fine. Don't fuss."

Marla bit her lip. "I'm sorry I upset you. You suspect Ryne of something, don't you?"

He turned off the tap, dried his hand and inspected the cut again. It was negligible. "I've no idea what the hell is going on with Ryne. And Zack's accident is still inexplicable."

"See? That proves my point. You have to deal with Ryne and all the problems we've been having. You don't have time for a mate. Especially one as young and inexperienced as this one is supposed to be." Marla placed her hand on his arm. "If anything, you need a woman who can stand by your side, someone strong who understands how the world works."

"I'll keep that in mind." He grabbed some paper towels intent on cleaning up the spilled coffee.

She smiled and then glanced away, a sad expression flickering over her face.

He paused, sensing there was something else she wanted to discuss. "Is something wrong, Marla?"

"Well, I hate to bother you."

"I'm your Alpha. If you have a problem, I'm here to help." He held back a sigh. Being Alpha required a lot of patience.

"Thank you, Kane. You're so good to me." She looked up at him and he was surprised to see a sheen of tears in her eyes.

"Marla?"

"It's just... Well, even though Ryne was acting strange, we'd been together for quite a while. We were close and I miss him." She wiped a tear from her cheek. "I don't have a lot of friends within the pack, or even in the human world for that matter. When I was with Ryne, I finally felt I belonged, like I had a home, someone who cared..."

Her voice trailed off and, without thinking, he reached out and hugged her. He knew what it was like to feel you didn't belong. "I miss Ryne, too."

She pressed her head to his chest and he patted her shoulders as she cried.

Helen entered the kitchen, looked at him comforting Marla and made a face. Like many in the pack, Helen had little patience with Marla.

"Kane, don't you have a meeting to go to?" Helen pulled out a frying pan and set it down on the stove with a bang.

Marla pulled away and wiped her damp cheeks. "I'm sorry, Kane. I'm keeping you from your work." She smoothed her hands over his chest. "And look at your shirt, its all wrinkled now."

"If it needs pressing, I can do it, Marla." Helen turned and folded her arms giving Marla a pointed stare.

"Of course you can, Helen. You're so good at all those menial little jobs." Marla smiled at the other woman and slowly withdrew her hands, her nails accidentally scraping lightly over his nipples.

He cleared his throat and stepped back. "Any time you need to talk, Marla—"

"She can come and see me." Helen interrupted.

"That's so sweet of you to offer." Marla turned and walked towards the door. "But Kane and I have a personal connection." She smiled at him again and then left.

"What was that about?" Helen went to the fridge and began to take items out, setting them on the counter.

"She was missing Ryne."

"Bull." She slammed the fridge door shut. "Marla is trying to get her claws into you. She sees herself as the next Alpha female."

He began to clean up the spill he'd made. "Don't be ridiculous. She was Ryne's girlfriend."

Helen snorted.

He watched the paper towel as it absorbed the coffee then cleared his throat. "I was wondering what you thought about the idea of me being mated to the girl from the Rock Valley pack. Everyone else has been giving me their opinion. You're one of the few who hasn't chimed in."

"And I'm not going to. It's your choice."

"That's not much help."

She shrugged. "I can give you some things to think about, but I'll not say yes or no to the matter."

"So what should I be thinking about?" He put the wet paper towels in the garbage.

"I won't ask if you love her, but do you like her? Are you attracted to her? Can you see yourself spending the rest of your life with her? Is there anyone else who interests you? What are the positives for the pack? What are the negatives?"

"Those are all the questions I've already been asking myself."

"And...?"

"I can already see that, as Alpha, I'll have very little time for myself. There's no one else I'm interested in and I don't have time to go looking for a mate. The union will be good for both packs, providing a strong alliance. Northern Oil has approached the Rock Valley pack as well as ours. We need to preserve our territory at all costs."

"It sounds to me like you've already made up your mind."

He nodded. "I'm thinking I'm going to do it."

Helen raised her brows but didn't say anything.

That evening, after delivering the news of his decision to the Council, he sat in his office and called an old friend.

"Hey Damien, how are you?"

"Kane?" Damien sounded surprised to hear from him. "I thought you'd be too busy doing Alpha stuff to bother with a lowly Enforcer like me."

He smiled at the good-natured teasing. "Yeah, well I have to step out of my tower and mingle with the commoners occasionally. Keeps me humble."

Damien snorted. "So how do you like being Alpha?"

"It's good. Demanding, but I'd expected that." He'd been the sole Beta for some time before Zack had added Ryne to help spread out the work. Eventually, he'd need to consider a co-Beta but was holding off in the hopes Ryne might come around, though that seemed less likely with each passing day.

"And Ryne?"

He felt himself stiffen. Damn, but Damien always did have the knack for cutting to the core of things. "I've no idea."

"Sorry." There was a pause. "That challenge caused quite a stir. Rumours are flying all over the place here."

"Really? Damn."

"Hey, it was brother against brother. That shit doesn't happen often. And the fact that it was two thirds of the Black Devils...well, we did gain some notoriety at the Academy."

"Yeah, I suppose." He rubbed his neck not happy that pack business was being bandied about Lycan Link.

"And when you let Ryne go..." Damien gave a low whistle. "I managed to see a copy of the report you sent in and your reasoning. Your interpretation of the Book of the Law, how you brought the various clauses together, it caught the attention of some of the big wigs. They're going to keep their eye on you."

"Wait a minute." One part of Damien's statement caught his attention. "How did you *manage* to see a copy of the report? They aren't for public record."

Damien laughed. "How do you think? There was this cute blonde working in the archives office and..." His voice trailed off suggestively.

"Never mind. I should have known." He shook his head. Damien liked the women a little too much. "You'll never settle for one female, will you?"

"Actually..."

Something in Damien's voice had him sitting up to listen. "What?"

"I've met this girl."

"And?"

"She's different. Her name is Beth and she has the most beautiful dove grey eyes."

"Nice."

"She's quiet. Not my usual type but there's something about her. I feel connected to her, protective. It kills me to be away from her."

"Sounds serious." Kane frowned as he listened, thinking Damien's description of his feelings for Beth were similar to his own towards Elise, even though they'd yet to meet.

"Yeah." Silence, then Damien sighed. "So, what about you?"

"Me? Well, that's why I'm calling. I'm being mated next week."

"What? No fucking way! Who is she?"

Kane chuckled. Damien's response was refreshing. As old friends, there was no deferring to rank, no motive behind his words. Just a pure, honest reply. "It's a political alliance. Her name is Elise Robinson and she's the Alpha's youngest daughter of the neighbouring pack."

"A political alliance? I didn't think packs did that shit anymore."

"She comes from a very traditional pack. Her father is old school. We've not actually met yet. I'm sort of pissed off about that." He frowned thinking how he'd instructed his Council of Elders to work on the other Alpha about arranging a meeting, even a short one, ahead of time.

"If you've not met, how will you know if you can get along together?"

"She's supposedly very quiet and biddable. We'll make it work."

"Better you than me."

He felt the need to justify himself. "It's for the good of the pack. We're battling increasing pressure from humans wanting to expand into our land."

Damien made a non-committal noise. "You always had a stronger sense of duty than the rest of us."

Duty. Well, that was what being an Alpha was about, wasn't it? He cleared his throat. "Anyway, I'm calling to invite you to the ceremony." He shared the date and time.

"Okay, I'll see what I can do. It all depends on whether my unit gets called out on a rescue mission though."

"Great. I'd really appreciate it if you could be there since Ryne..." His voice trailed off.

"Understood. I still can't believe Ryne did that."

Part of him wanted to share the problems the pack had been having and the evidence Marla had presented that implicated Ryne in Zack's crash. But did he really want to smear Ryne's reputation with his friend before gaining conclusive proof? A part of him still hoped there was an explanation for what was going on, an explanation that didn't point to his brother.

He hoped he wasn't being too big of a fool.

Chapter 9

Kane and the Council of Elders arrived at Alpha Robinson's house early in the day. There were a number of formalities to be completed, fine details to be hashed out, papers to be signed. Jake, the pack Beta, seemed a decent sort but the Alpha was still reserved and hard to get to know.

When they finally left off negotiations for a break, Kane sought out his future father-in-law.

"I'm curious, where is Elise?" He'd been waiting for her to join them but, two hours later, there was still no sign of his soon-to-be mate.

"She'll be here." The Alpha assured him. "She's not interested in pack politics."

"And yet she's agreed to be an Alpha's mate." He murmured.

"She'll be fine. You've no need to worry she'll embarrass you."

"That wasn't my concern." He tried to explain himself, wondering if the man was being purposely obtuse. "I'd like to meet her, talk to her. Ensure she's fine with this."

"I've left a message for her to come here as soon as she gets home but don't worry. She's my daughter. She'll do her duty."

'Do her duty.' It sounded like at least they'd have that in common. About to ask another question, a

door opened near the rear of the room and he turned to see Elise enter.

His wolf rumbled its approval and he did the same. She looked just as he remembered. Long legs, a trim waist, nice breasts. Her lips were plump and he wondered what it would be like to kiss her.

Their gazes locked and he was once again struck by her wide, green eyes. She flushed under his intense scrutiny and he tried to give her a reassuring smile before turning to comment to her father.

"I see she's arrived."

The Alpha turned and sighed. "And she's been out for a run again."

"Is that a problem?" He cocked his head.

"I specifically asked her to stay close to the house today." He shook his head. "Give me a minute to speak with her before you come over, please."

"Of course. I need to speak to your Elders again to clarify a point."

A few minutes later, he turned to observe the father-daughter dynamics that were occurring across the room. Elise didn't look happy and he suspected she was getting a scolding; the Alpha didn't seem the type to take kindly to having his orders ignored.

What was being said? He had to actively make himself not tune in to the conversation with his keen Lycan hearing. It was decidedly bad manners to eavesdrop and Lycans kept their keen senses under control in most circumstances so those around them had a modicum of privacy.

He clasped his hands behind his back and waited.

Elise looked his way, her expression less than pleased. Did she not know why he was here? He'd expressly said... He held back a growl. It would seem somewhere along the lines his wishes had been ignored.

Perhaps Elise and her father had more in common than they realized; both following instructions only when it suited them.

She turned away and argued some point, then her shoulders slumped. Tightening his lips, Kane decided to join them. At the last minute, he schooled his features into a more pleasant expression not wanting her to think he was finding fault with her.

"This must be your beautiful daughter I've been hearing so much about." He smiled at her but she didn't respond, seeming lost in thought.

"Elise!" Her father spoke sharply and she gave a start.

"I'm pleased to meet you, Elise." He tried again, keeping his eyes steady on hers as he held out his hand.

"Er...hello." She didn't take his hand until her father gave her a nudge.

He smiled as he enveloped her small hand in his, a tingle of sexual awareness shooting up his arm. "I think we will suit each other." He nodded to her father and then gave her hand a squeeze. "I'll see you later at the ceremony." After flicking a look over the length of her again, he nodded and headed back to where the councils were meeting.

His departure might have been abrupt but the feel of her soft skin and her intoxicating scent were swamping his senses, causing his body to harden and his wolf to pace restlessly. Better to leave than embarrass himself.

The afternoon passed quickly with negotiations being completed but no further sign of Elise though he seemed to be the only one concerned about that point.

"It's not unusual," William reassured him. "In ages past, you wouldn't have even seen her until the ceremony. Don't push the Alpha too much. He's a stickler for tradition and with Northern Oil breathing down our necks, we need this alliance."

Kane nodded. Maybe it was his own nerves that had him questioning what was going on. After all, spending an entire day in another wolf's pack house was enough to set any Alpha on edge. Even as a welcome guest, his inner wolf was watchful, assessing those around them. Damien had sent him a message saying he wouldn't be able to attend; maybe if his friend had been there he would have been more at ease. It would have been nice to have a member of the Black Devils watching his back.

Dinner was announced and they entered a large dining area with a long harvest table big enough to seat all the guests. Fall flowers and fine china decorated the table while meat, vegetables and fresh rolls sat ready to be served. It was a spread that even Helen would have approved of had she been there.

Elise slid into the chair beside him and he gave her a nod in greeting. Speeches were given throughout the meal so there was no room for conversation. He did his best to appear interested in each speaker while casting side-long looks at her. She was picking at her food, only occasionally glancing up to scan the crowd, often focusing on the far corner. He followed the direction of her gaze and saw a young man with brown hair glaring at him. Had the boy had his hopes set on Elise?

Kane eyed his soon-to-be mate. She was pale, her hands clasped tightly in her lap as she nodded at the server who removed her plate. The meal was over and he'd not noticed her eating even a bite. Was it just nerves or something more? Before he could decide, they were called to the front.

He stood and offered her his arm. She took a deep breath, lifted her chin and joined him.

All eyes were on them as they took their place before her father. As Alpha, he'd preside over the ceremony.

"Clasp each other's hands and extend them over the Book of the Law."

Kane took Elise's hand. It felt cold and trembled slightly. He rubbed his thumb over the back, trying to offer some comfort.

Her father began to speak. "From the moment of first transformation when a Lycan meets its inner wolf, the two become a single unit, one and yet distinct. They are joined in a way that cannot be separated; living together, sharing thoughts and feelings, each dependent on the other for survival. But such a union is not enough. Lycans were not made to be alone. They require a mate to share their life, to procreate, to build a pack."

The Alpha looked at those gathered. "It is for this reason representatives of our pack have gathered. Tonight, under the light of the moon, a sacred symbol given to us by the gods, we assemble to witness this union. Are there any opposed?"

Kane watched as Elise bit her lip and half turned. He did the same and noticed the same young man again. There was no doubt the fellow wasn't happy yet he made no protest.

Inwardly Kane's wolf sneered. *He is but a pup.*

When no one spoke, the Alpha continued. "Kane and Elise, tonight you are formally mated, before your pack, under the light of the gods. As mates, you must put the needs of the other before your own, work together in partnership for the good of the pack and raise your pups to know the ways of our people."

He took out a leather cord and began to tie their wrists together, wrapping it in an intricate pattern. "This cord that binds you together represents the strength of your bond, a bond that will last until death. Once it is knotted you are no longer two but one, accepting no other mate, faithful and supportive. Do you agree?"

Kane nodded. "I do."

Elise wet her lips and then replied in a whisper. "I do."

"Then so be it." The Alpha completed tying the knot, giving it a firm tug before stepping back. "It is done. Kane and Elise, you are mates."

Applause filled the room, even a few howls. Some reached out to pat Kane on the back, while others congratulated Elise. Finally, they managed to exit the pack house and he gave a sigh of relief. It was good to be outside. The room had been warm and his wolf had been restless surrounded by the scents of the other pack.

A cabin had been set up for them so they could consummate their relationship before heading back home tomorrow. He'd tried to negotiate this out of the agreement thinking it would be better if they had more time to get to know each other, but the Elders of her pack had been adamant. Why, he wasn't sure. It wasn't like he'd change his mind and send her back.

They walked along, hands tied together, the moon lighting the path. He felt he should say something but was oddly tongue-tied. Their footsteps crunched on the gravel path, crickets chirring in the background as they approached the cabin.

It was an older building made of logs and surrounded by trees on three sides. Their feet thumped on the wooden porch and he cursed to himself as he fumbled with the door latch; his dominant hand was still tied to Elise's. When the door opened, he wondered if he should attempt to carry her over the threshold human-fashion. He dismissed the idea almost as soon as he thought of it. No, she might not appreciate the gesture.

Instead, he stepped aside so she could enter first and followed her close behind.

After turning on the light, he looked around taking in the small kitchenette, eating area and a sofa in front of a fireplace. There was a door to the left that likely led to a bedroom and bathroom.

"Well." His voice sounded unusually loud after the silence between them.

Elise gave a start, her eyes seeming wider than usual.

He gave a soft and hopefully encouraging smile. "The first order of business would be to remove this, wouldn't you say?" He held up their joined wrists and she nodded in agreement. Pulling a pocketknife from his pocket, he followed tradition and cut the rope. Untying the knot was considered bad luck, a symbol their bond wasn't strong enough to withstand outside influences.

Elise pulled her arm away and rubbed her wrist as did he. The rope hadn't been tied that tightly but his skin was still irritated from it.

"We have a similar reaction to being imprisoned, I see." He nodded towards the action of her hands.

"Yes." She didn't elaborate and silence stretched between them again.

Damn this was awkward. He rubbed his neck and stared around the room, not quite sure what to do or say. Hopping into the sack and having sex with someone who was obviously nervous around him wasn't an easy thing to negotiate. "It's getting late. Would you like to use the bathroom first?"

"All right."

He watched her leave the room and sighed. Yeah, awkward to the nth degree.

The leather tie was on the ground where it had fallen and he picked it up, fingering the soft material.

Usually the female saved the tie as a memento of the occasion, but Elise hadn't even looked at it. Had he made a mistake agreeing to this? She hadn't said anything, hadn't protested and yet...

He put the tie on the table. It was an important symbol to him and, he hoped, one day Elise would feel the same.

Chapter 10

Kane paced the small bedroom, listening to the sounds of Elise in the shower. His mental image of her naked, water cascading over her curves, had his body uncomfortably hard while his inner wolf pushed against the constraints he kept it under.

Our mate is nearby. We need to claim her.

"Soon," he murmured. "We can't just jump her."

A blood-bond is needed, the wolf insisted. *Then she will be ours and no one can ever take her.*

"No, not yet," he told the animal. "When we blood-bond it will be because she loves me just as I..." He didn't finish the sentence, shying away from the word. It was too soon. He didn't, couldn't, love her. Not yet. It was desire talking, no more. He cleared his throat and continued.

"We need to go slowly."

Nothing is to be gained by waiting here though.

Perhaps the animal was right. If he went to her, it might be easier. With a nod, he started to strip, only to hear the water being turned off.

Should he go in or wait here?

And if he waited here, should he be in bed or—

Before he could decide the door opened and Elise appeared. Steam from the shower swirled around her and his imagination took a flight of fancy, seeing her as an angel stepping out of a cloud.

For a moment they stared at each other, his gaze sweeping over her, the light from the bathroom turning her nightgown into a gossamer transparency. It allowed him an enticing glimpse of her curves.

Suddenly he noticed her hands were clenched into fists and she was nervously biting her lip. Damn, he was ogling her like an idiot. He cleared his throat.

"Hi."

"Hi." She replied back, a faint tremble in her voice.

Yeah, this was still damned awkward. He took a deep breath and walked over to where she stood.

She flicked a look at him and then focused to some point behind him, not meeting his gaze.

"Elise," he placed his hands on her shoulders. "I know this isn't easy for you. If it makes you feel any better, it's new to me, too."

She let out a soft gasp and stared up a him. "You mean you've never...?"

"No! I have. Many times."

Her eyes widened and he silently cursed himself.

"I mean..." He paused and took a deep breath. What the hell did he mean? He was usually more eloquent than this. "What I was trying to say, very ineptly, is I've never been mated before. Being mates is new to both of us, but we'll figure it out together. Okay?"

He gave her crooked smile and she nodded.

"However, as for...consummating...our union, I *do* know what I'm doing. I'll be gentle, I promise."

He reached out and touched her upper arms. She trembled but didn't try to pull away so he ran his hands up and down her arms marvelling at the feel of her. She seemed so tiny and delicate compared to himself. "You're a slight little thing, aren't you?"

"I...yes."

He could feel her muscles tense under his palms. Damn. There really was no easy way around the fact they had to consummate their relationship tonight.

"I'm going to kiss you now, okay?"

She nodded and he trailed his lips down her neck. A shiver ran through her and he smiled at her reaction. She wasn't averse to his touch.

He encircled her waist with his hands, pulling her close until they were touching from chest to knee.

"Mmm, you're so soft." Rumbling his approval, he kissed her, brushing lips over hers, smiling when she responded. He deepened the kiss, stroking her tongue, advancing and retreating until she joined in the gentle duel.

The taste of her, the scent of her, it consumed him, stoking the fire that already burned within. Unable to wait, he picked her up and carried her to the bed…

Kane's mind was blank, his muscles limp. He drifted, satiated and content. Had there ever been a better feeling than this?

Slowly, he became aware of his surroundings; the pounding of his heart, the moonlight streaming in the window, the softness of his mate pressed close beside him.

A smile curved his lips. He turned his head, planning to say their mating had been the best sex he'd ever had only to have the words freeze on his lips.

A tear was trickling down Elise's cheek.

The sight was like ice water being thrown on him, the feeling of contentment from moments ago swept away in the wake of concern for his mate.

He reached out and caught the droplet with his finger. "I'm sorry, Elise."

"It doesn't matter." She answered quietly, still staring at the ceiling. "It couldn't be helped."

He wondered what she was referring to. The pain of losing her virginity or the fact they hadn't been given the time to get to know each other first? Both had been out of their control.

"No, it couldn't," he sighed heavily. He slipped his arm around her waist and drew her closer. She let her cheek rest against his muscular chest. The feel of her nestled to his side had his wolf murmuring its approval. "I wish I could have given you more time to get to know me but the Elders wanted our union sealed immediately."

She didn't answer, merely nodding.

Should he continue the conversation? Press her to speak? Or was it better to remain silent and tackle the topic later? He pressed his lips together, deciding to follow her lead and returned to staring at the ceiling, one arm over his head, the other wrapped protectively around his new mate.

When he woke the next morning, he spent some time watching Elise sleep. She was on her side, one hand tucked under her cheek, her lips slightly parted. There were pink marks on her skin, evidence of what they'd shared. The memory had his body stirring and if it wasn't that they had to get on the road soon, he could have stayed in bed with her all day.

Instead, he rolled out of bed, showered and dressed then wandered into the kitchenette. Thankfully someone had thought to stock it with the basics and he made himself a cup coffee.

Their bonding rope was still sitting on the table where he'd set it the night before. He turned it over and over in his hand before tucking it away in his duffle bag. When he got home, he'd save it in the small wooden box on his dresser where he kept his cufflinks and a watch with a wolf's head embossed on the face.

Zack had given him the watch on the night of his first transformation. Up until now, it had been his most treasured possession, marking the day he'd met his inner wolf. But now, now he'd met his mate and the bit of leather would always remind him of the life-changing moment. The only thing that could top this would be the day he and Elise blood-bonded.

Smiling at that thought, he stepped outside and leaned on the railing. Dawn was just breaking, the best time of the day in his opinion. Birds chirping, the sun's rays spilling across the sky, the ground damp from dew and the air still heavy and scent-laden. It wasn't his territory though and the sight didn't fill him with the usual feeling of peace and purpose. He'd be glad to get on the road and back to his home.

The sound of the shower alerted him to the fact that Elise was awake so he decided to prepare breakfast then went to greet her.

"Good morning, Elise. I heard you in the shower when I came in, so I made some breakfast for us."

"Oh. Thanks."

He extended his arm, ushering her into the kitchenette. He'd set the table and prepared bacon and eggs, juice and toast. "I wasn't sure what you liked to eat, but this is what I can cook. I hope it's suitable."

"You cooked this?"

Her expression had him chuckling as he helped her with her chair. "Yes. I am capable of fending for myself, you know. And, I can't have you undernourished. People might think I don't know how to take care of you." He pressed a kiss on her cheek and gave her a casual caress before sitting down across from her.

She'd not spoken much yet so he decided to devote the meal to trying to get to know her better.

"We'll need to take a few days to get used to each other, to become acquainted with various likes and dislikes. Is there anything you aren't fond of eating?"

"Um...not really."

Not the most enlightening response but at least she was talking. He plowed on. "Good. I'll eat almost anything myself. Do you like to read? Watch movies?"

Her responses were short at first, but eventually she seemed to relax and began to expand on her answers. He felt his own inner tension begin to ease. They were finally making some progress.

"Our territories adjoin and with our packs under an alliance, we technically have miles and miles of forest to roam in now." He leaned back, a cup of coffee in his hand. "Personally, I love a good run over rugged terrain. How about you? When I first saw you, it was apparent that you'd just come in from exercising."

"Yes, I'd been out with...a friend." Her smile faded.

He recalled the young man and struggled to keep his voice calm. "And this...friend...would he be the young male who was shooting daggers at me yesterday? Tall with sandy hair, and about twenty years of age?"

"Yes. That was Bryan. He had hoped to speak to my father about being my...mate." She looked away.

He could see a sheen of tears forming in her eyes and a cold heavy feeling filled his gut. "And you? How did you feel about that?"

She looked down and answered softly. "I...I was hoping for the same thing."

"I see." He was silent, cursing under his breath. He'd had his suspicions. Damn, why hadn't he pressed harder for an opportunity to talk to her ahead of time? Because he'd allowed his infatuation with her to cloud his judgement, that's why.

And yet, his wolf asked, *would you have been willing to walk away and let that pup have her?*

He knew he wouldn't. Call it arrogance but he knew she was meant to be his and he wouldn't give her up. Knowing that, how should he respond to her?

Sighing heavily, he spoke. "I'm not surprised. You're a beautiful female and it would be strange if no one in your pack had wanted you." He chose his words carefully. "You know, Elise, sometimes our lives have moments of great disappointment. It's difficult at the time, but we have to move beyond." He reached across the table and put a finger under her chin, forcing her to look up at him. "Our being mated was of great importance to the well-being of both our packs. It's our duty to them to make this work, agreed?" He gazed into her eyes, willing her to agree.

A beat passed then another. Concern rose within him. If she balked at the idea...

She nodded.

He gave no outward sign of his relief but his inner wolf was pleased.

Already we are of one accord. The animal lifted its chin.

In some areas, he cautioned. But we can't expect everything to go smoothly.

If we blood-bond with her...

When the time is right, he murmured.

The wolf slid him a look of disgust but he paid it no mind. Standing he extended his hand to Elise and pulled her to her feet.

"Thank you." He kissed her forehead and then tucked a loose strand of hair behind her ear. She was so beautiful, his mate; it was all he could do to step away. He knew however, he needed to give her time and space, not push too much, let her find her own way.

"I need to meet with the Elders but should only be half an hour. When I get back, will you go on a run with me and give me a tour of your land?"

"Okay."

He couldn't resist and gave her a passionate, branding kiss before quickly leaving. If he'd stayed, he knew he would have dragged her back to bed.

Chapter 11

He kept his final meeting with the Rock Valley council as short as possible. Their traditional pack didn't suit him and he knew Elise was waiting for him. He'd rather spend time with her.

Thinking of the kiss he'd given her before leaving, he headed to the edge of the woods anticipating more of the same. However, as he approached, he found the pup, Bryan, stroking his mate's face! If he'd been less civilized, he would have shifted and grabbed the boy by the scruff of the neck and killed him for daring to touch her.

He paused a few feet away fighting for control. They were so intent on their conversation, they hadn't even noticed him. It was another indication the pup was inferior. A male worthy of Elise would be aware of his surroundings, ready to protect her at a moment's notice.

Purposely, he stepped on a twig causing it to snap. The sound made them both give a start of surprise and the pup jumped away from Elise, a sure sign of guilt.

"Elise, I'm glad you found a way to keep yourself occupied while I was finishing off pack business." He didn't try to hide the angry growl in his voice.

"I...I was just talking to Bryan," she stammered, stepping back.

"So I see." Kane shot her a brief glance, and then focused his attention on the interloper. "This is the...friend...you spoke of this morning?"

"Yes, this is Bryan. We've been friends since we were pups."

"I'm glad you had someone to keep you company while you were waiting. However," he narrowed his eyes, "it would do your 'friend' well to remember that you are now *my* mate and off limits to all others."

Elise tried to defend her actions. "We were just talking, nothing else."

"I do not appreciate other males standing quite so close when...talking...to my mate." The words rumbled from his throat and Bryan retreated. Kane curled his lips at the show of subservience.

"Elise, I'd better go. I...I'll see you around." Bryan gave Elise another look then turned and left, his inner wolf no doubt telling him retreat was advisable.

"Yes, I'll see you around." Elise responded softly. Once he was gone, she turned, brows lowered, fists clenched. "You didn't need to chase him off like that."

"I didn't chase him off. I merely let him know that you are my mate now and a proper distance needs to be maintained."

"He was just—"

"I know what he was 'just' doing," he interrupted. "I could sense his desire for you and I do not share my mate with anyone. We are bonded and you are mine. No other male is allowed to sniff around you."

"Sniff around me?" Her eyes opened wide, her mouth in a perfect outraged 'O'.

"Yes. That boy needs to remember you are off limits before he makes a grave mistake." He knew he was being dictatorial but he didn't care. The Alpha wolf in him was staking its claim.

Elise huffed, folding her arms. "Kane, you—"

"Elise, this conversation is over. You are my mate. Bryan will stay away. End of topic. Now, are we going for a run or not?"

She pursed her lips and he wouldn't have been surprised if she declined. When she gave a nod and shifted forms, he was pleased she wasn't going to draw out the fight. Some things he was willing to compromise on but not this.

He shifted to his wolf form and followed, content to let her take the lead. There were times to push and times to sit back and wait; this was one of the latter. Plus, it was interesting to see how she and her wolf worked together.

His mate was fast, leaping over logs, skirting around trunks, quickly adjusting her path and pace to suit the terrain. At some point, she began to increase her pace and he sensed she was testing him. Seamlessly, he adjusted his pace to hers, maintaining the same distance between them regardless of how many times she changed her pace.

Perhaps the fact she hadn't bested him yet was what caused her to veer off the path heading for rougher terrain. She took them down a slope, over a stream and up the opposite bank. It was as she was about to leap over a pile of brush that a scent caught his attention. With a burst of speed, he slammed into her, the momentum knocking her to the ground with him landing on top of her. He pressed his teeth to her throat to end her instinctive struggles.

When she finally stilled, he released his hold. As one they shifted back to human form and she glared at him, her breathing heavy.

"Why did you do that?" She panted.

"There's a leg trap directly ahead of you. A few more yards and you would have stepped in it."

Elise turned and scanned the area ahead of her. He could tell the moment she spotted the trap by the shudder that passed over her.

He was thankful he'd been at the pack house that morning when the scouts had reported in. "Poachers were seen in the area. We're near the edge of the property so I was on the lookout. Rest here for a minute. I'm going to spring that one and then see what else I can find."

"I'm coming with you." She stood and he was pleased she wasn't the kind to cower at the first sign of problems.

"Fine, but stay behind me." He searched for a sturdy stick and then used it to trigger the trap. It was an older model, with sharp metal teeth designed to dig into the flesh of any creature unfortunate enough to step in it. Elise jumped as the trap sprang shut, snapping the stick in two and he gave her a meaningful look. That could have been her leg.

For the next half hour, they scoured the edge of the property, discovering four more traps. Satisfied he'd done a complete search, he gathered the traps into a pile and marked the location so they could be collected later. There was no point in leaving them for the hunters to reset.

"We'll report this to your father when we return and he can send another set of scouts out to check further afield."

"Thank you." Elise touched his arm.

"For what?"

"For stopping me. I could have snapped a bone if I'd stepped in one of those."

"I'm your Alpha now. It's my job to watch out for everyone in the pack, but especially you. As my mate, you're the most important member to me." He stared at her intently and she flushed.

"Yes, but I should have been watching more carefully where I was going. I know these woods. I...I wasn't paying attention."

"What were you thinking about instead?"

She hesitated before answering. "You, or to be more precise, I guess I was testing you to see if you'd keep up."

He grinned and drew her close for a quick kiss. "Rest assured, Elise, no matter what you dish out, I will keep up with you."

They shifted back into wolf form and this time he led the way to the edge of the woods. When they arrived at the cabin, Elise headed inside while he went to the main house to tell her father about the traps. By the time he returned, she was asleep no doubt tired from the events of the past twenty-four hours. They'd have to leave soon but he let her rest while he showered.

He'd just toweled off and was getting dressed when a sound behind him drew his attention. Elise was waking up, her hair tousled, her eyes still heavy with sleep.

"I see you're awake."

"Uh-huh. What time is it?" She rubbed her eyes.

"Almost noon. You must have been tired after our run." He turned and grabbed a shirt only to pause when he noticed her frowning.

"What happened to your side?"

He shrugged, knowing she was referring to the scar from the challenge. While Lycans healed quickly, there was still a noticeable mark. "Nothing. Just a scratch from a fight."

"That's more than a scratch. Who was the fight with?" She pressed for more information much to his annoyance.

"Another werewolf named Ryne." He gave the minimal amount of information, hoping she'd let the matter go. Luck wasn't on his side.

She dug deeper, obviously wanting details. "Why were you fighting?"

"You aren't going to leave this alone, are you?" He finished dressing then turned to face her, arms folded.

"No. I have an inquiring mind."

For a moment, he considered not telling her but she'd find out sooner or later. It was better she heard the news from him rather than garnering bits and pieces from blown-out-of-proportion gossip. He walked to the window and stared outside while speaking, trying to keep the recount factual and unemotional even though the memory still cut deep. "As you know, I'm the new Alpha of my pack. Our previous leader, Zack, was killed in an accident. Ryne and I were both Betas. Some of the pack favoured me as the new Alpha and others wanted Ryne."

"So, it went to a pack vote?"

"Usually that's what would have happened, but Ryne pulled out the old rules and declared a challenge."

"A challenge? That's not done anymore. It's ridiculous! We've evolved beyond that." Elise shuddered and he understood her reaction.

"I agree, but he was still within his rights."

"So...what happened?"

"We fought. I won." His fists clenched as he recalled the experience.

"Did you...kill him?"

He could tell she was appalled at the idea and was pleased he could ease her fears. "No. It was a long drawn out fight and both of us were pretty beaten up by the time it was over. He made an impulsive move. I pinned him down and could have crushed his windpipe, but instead let him go."

"And where is he now? Did he stay in the pack?"

He shook his head. "Ryne chose to leave. I told him he could stay—we'd been packmates for years—but he said he wasn't going to grovel in front of me. He was bitter and said some crazy things." Why he'd omitted to mention Ryne was his half-brother, he wasn't sure. Perhaps it was because that wound was still especially sensitive. He gave what he hoped was a negligent shrug, but knew, despite his efforts, the tone of his voice when he spoke belied his outward lack of concern. "In the long run, it's probably best he's gone. There would have been too much division in the pack if he'd stayed."

"And is the pack united behind you now? Even Ryne's supporters?"

"Yes. The pack mentality still runs through all of our blood. The strongest member is the leader and we instinctively accept that." He raised his chin as he spoke. "I proved myself. The others are at peace with the results."

He turned to look at her, curious what her reaction would be to the story.

She gave him a slight smile. "I'm glad you won and that you healed well from your fight."

"Thanks." His heart warmed at her concern and his wolf murmured its approval.

She already has some feeling for us.

He gave a barely perceptible nod. Her reaction had mattered to him more than he thought it would. However, it wasn't a topic he wanted to dwell on. "It was a while ago—all water under the bridge now." Picking up his watch, he checked the time. "You need to get up and get dressed. We'll be leaving in about an hour."

"Leaving?" She sounded surprised.

"Yes. I need to return to my pack. It's only about an hour's drive but I want to get back in good time so that you can see your new home before it's dark."

Chapter 12

Kane stood by his truck, the passenger door open so he could help Elise inside. The back was loaded with boxes of her things. All that was needed was for her to finish her goodbyes. He watched the interaction with interest. Every pack's dynamics were different.

The Beta's wife seemed to be the equivalent of Helen, running the pack house and handing out motherly advice. She was fussing over Elise, fixing her hair as a mother might before sending a child off to school for the day, reminding her to come visit before giving her a hug and passing her off to Jake.

Jake, the Beta, must have had a close relationship with Elise. He gave her a one-armed hug, then kept her there as Elise rested her head against his chest. She appeared to take an extra deep breath as if being near the man provided comfort.

Kane cocked his head. Had the Beta assumed a fatherly role in Elise's life? It would make sense given the Alpha seemed distant and withdrawn.

"I'll miss you, Jake." There was an unmistakable sadness in Elise's voice causing Kane to once again wonder if he'd made a mistake. The past couldn't be changed though. They were mates now and he wasn't going to let her go.

The Beta kissed the top of Elise's head and she turned to her father next. She stood before him, an awkwardness filling the space between them before he gave her a stiff hug and whispered something to her. She nodded and pulled away.

With a strained smile on her face, she descended the steps and climbed into the truck. Kane closed the door and rounded the vehicle while Elise gave a final wave.

"All set?"

She nodded and he started the truck. Her chin was trembling and he opened his mouth to speak but there was nothing he could say that would make the parting easier. It was better to get it over with. His hands gripped the steering wheel and he sighed, put the truck in gear and drove away.

He tried to start a conversation with comments about the weather, the scenery, a humorous billboard they passed but Elise seemed disinclined to talk. To fill the silence, he flipped on the radio letting the music make up for the lack of discussion. A sideways glance showed Elise with her head leaning against the window, staring blankly at the passing landscape.

His lips tightened as he recalled what it was like to leave a place he'd considered home. It had happened all too often when he'd been younger. His father had been a throwback, a rogue who could never settle down or integrate into a pack. They'd been constantly on the move for one reason or another. Either they'd be kicked out because his father's volatile temper had offended someone or the man would decide it was time for a new adventure. Whatever the case, his own young heart would ache as they drove away.

That feeling would be what Elise was experiencing and now he was the cause. Silently, he vowed he'd make it up to her, teach her to love her new home, assure her he'd always be there for her and she'd never have to leave again. He wouldn't be the kind of mate his father had been.

Eventually Elise came out of her reverie and sat up straighter beside him.

"How large is your pack?"

He smiled, pleased she was willing to talk. The tension in his muscles eased. "About the same size as the one you grew up in. Our Alpha house has six bedrooms and four baths, office space, a living room, a large dining area and a kitchen. The basement was recently renovated and is a multi-purpose room for meetings with a media centre, pool table, and play area for the young ones."

"It sounds nice. Who shares the house with you?"

"Besides yourself?" He grinned over at her before returning his attention to the road. "My Beta is John and his mate's name is Carrie. They're expecting their first in a few months. Zack's widow—he was the previous Alpha—she's continued to stay there as well. Her name is Helen."

Elise nodded. "There are always people in and out of our house—I mean my father's house. Is yours similar?"

"Yeah, sometimes it's a three-ring circus. With you arriving, it will probably be especially busy as everyone will want to stop by to meet you." He noticed she bit her lip, waves of wariness coming off her. He reached over and clasped her knee. "It will be fine. We're not as...traditional...as your old pack. They're a friendly bunch and will be happy to meet you."

He continued to offer explanations, mentioning various pack members and their roles. "Don't worry, I know all this information is going over your head but at least you'll have heard some of the names when you meet face to face."

"Thanks."

"I think you'll like the territory. It's heavily wooded with streams that feed a small lake. We even have a waterfall due to glacier-cut ravines. It's one of the largest on the west coast." He couldn't help the pride that crept into his voice as he spoke.

"I've heard your pack has a lot of influence."

"*Our* pack, Elise." He corrected. "You're Alpha female now."

He noted the news had her clenching her hands in her lap.

"You'll do fine in the role. Your father was Alpha."

"Right." She looked down at her hands. "Confession time. I never had much to do with the running of the pack or the politics involved. I was the baby of the family." She shrugged and made a face. "It never interested me that much. Sometimes, I helped with filing but that's about it."

"I didn't agree to be mated with you because I needed a secretary. Helen and Carrie will help you learn the ropes."

"I suppose."

A dinging sound from the dashboard interrupted the conversation.

"Looks like we need to get gas. There's a place on the edge of town. I have to stop at the hardware store as well."

As quickly as possible, he completed his errands. Now that he was back on home turf, his mind was full of the long list of things he had to do. He'd been away for almost forty-eight hours and, while John was in charge during his absence, there always seemed to be things that needed the Alpha's exclusive attention. Elise would understand that, though. Even if she hadn't been involved in running the pack, she'd be aware of how busy her father had always been.

He stowed his purchases in the back of the truck and climbed back into the cab.

"Sorry to keep you waiting."

"That's okay. I was people watching while you were gone."

"Smythston is a nice place. Not too big but large enough that it has the needed amenities. People aren't too nosey either which is a bonus. I'll have to bring you in to town one day and show you around."

"That sounds nice."

He nodded. "Just a few more miles and we'll be home."

The news had Elise looking tense again and he gave her knee a reassuring pat once more before putting both hands back on the steering wheel. They were on the part of the road where Zack had his accident, the memory of the crash making him more cautious. It was still hard to believe Zack was gone and that it was because someone had tampered with his brakes. Trying, once again, to figure out that mystery kept him quiet until they pulled up in front of the house.

As he brought the truck to a stop, the front door of the sprawling house opened and several people came out to greet them.

"Welcome home, Kane."

"Congratulations on being mated."

"We missed you."

The friendly comments swirled around him and it took him some time to make his way around to Elise's side of the truck. By the time he got there, she was already out and waiting for him. He wrapped his arm around her shoulders.

"Everyone, this is Elise, my mate."

His announcement drew everyone's attention and they took a moment to size her up, nodding in approval.

Carrie stepped forward first, a hand on her rounded belly. "Hello, Elise. I'm Carrie. Welcome to our pack."

"And I'm John, her mate, and Kane's Beta."

"I'm pleased to meet you." Elise smiled and shook their hands and then greeted the others.

Pleased with how Elise was already making friends, Kane grabbed two of her bags from the vehicle and then gestured with his chin. "Come on inside. The others will bring the rest of your things."

A few of the men immediately headed towards the truck, grabbing the remaining boxes. He nodded in approval at how everyone was pitching in to help Elise feel welcome.

He led the way inside, knowing the rest would follow. The familiar scents and sounds of the house washed over him and he exhaled happily. It was good to be home.

"Kane?" Marla appeared beside him.

"Yes?" He hadn't noticed her outside greeting Elise but he must have missed her in the crowd.

"Kane, I need to talk to you." She placed her hand on his arm.

"Can it wait? I just got home." He held up the bags he was still holding.

"Oh. I...I'm sorry. I just..." She pressed her lips together and blinked back tears.

He sighed and set down Elise's bags. "I guess I can spare you a minute."

"Oh, thank you so much, Kane." Marla placed her hand on his chest. "I...I missed you."

"Marla..."

"I know you have a mate now. We can still be friends though, right? You know how it is for me." She gave a sad smile. "With Ryne gone and no family..."

Guilt washed over him as she mentioned not having a family. He still felt responsible for the death of her father. It had been years ago and everyone said there'd been nothing he could do but that did little to ease his sense of guilt. He and Dietrich had been out on patrols together and, being the senior Lycan, Dietrich had taken the lead. For some reason, the man had veered from the usual route into more dangerous territory and lost his footing, tumbling down a ravine and breaking his neck. To this day, Kane wondered if he could have prevented the accident.

He realized he hadn't really been listening to what Marla was saying. And, he glanced over Marla's shoulder and noticed Elise was standing near the base of the stairs looking lost. "Elise, wait! I'll just be a minute."

Marla tugged at his arm. "But Kane, I need to tell you about Ryne and—"

"Yes, I know you miss him." He nodded, impatient to get away.

"But there's more. He—"

"Marla, we'll talk later. Elise is waiting for me."

"I'm sorry. I know I'm a bother." She let her hand fall and stared down at the ground. "I'll be fine. Just forget what I said."

He sighed. "Marla, you're not a bother. As a member of the pack, you're always welcome to approach me. It's just your timing that's off."

She leaned into him. "You're so good to me, Kane."

He absent-mindedly gave her a one-armed hug. "Anytime, Marla."

"I'll hold you to that." She suddenly brightened. "Now go take care of your new little friend. You really shouldn't keep her waiting. She might get bored and go looking elsewhere." With a laugh, she turned and walked away.

He frowned watching her walk away. Why would she make a comment like that? Of course, Elise wouldn't get bored. Giving his head a shake, he made his way to Elise who was patiently waiting for him.

"Sorry about that. Marla needed a bit of reassurance." He took her hand and led her upstairs, guiding her to their suite at the end of a small corridor.

"Our rooms are up here. Since the house is usually busy, I have my own little retreat. There's a bedroom, bath and a sitting room that are strictly off limits to the rest of the pack. Sometimes, even social animals like wolves need their own space." He offered the explanation with a crooked smile, while opening the door and ushering her inside.

"It's very nice." Elise wandered about the room, peering into the closet and then into the sitting room.

"Carrie moved some of my stuff over, so there'll be room for your things. She'll help you unpack or rearrange anything that you want."

"Thanks, but I can do it myself. If she's going to whelp soon, I'm sure she's tired and doesn't need the extra work."

"That's considerate of you." He guided her to the window to show her the view thinking it would be a pleasant surprise for her. "See over to the west? That's the direction of your father's land. Of course, you can't see it, but possibly it will make your old pack seem not quite so far away."

She seemed pleased and looked up at him with a smile. He turned her so she was facing him and he cupped her face, his thumb stroking her cheek. "I know this has been hard on you, Elise. Leaving behind everything you know on such short notice has to have been a bit overwhelming, but I'm proud of how you're handling things."

"I think I'm sort of...in shock, maybe?" She furrowed her brow. "Everything happened so fast that I didn't have time to think or react. I just instinctively followed the Alpha's orders." She shrugged and sighed. "Besides, there really wasn't much choice was there? I could fall in with the plan or leave the pack."

"You're right. A wolf that refuses to comply with the Alpha doesn't stay in the pack long, though I doubt your father would have immediately thrown you out."

"Maybe not right away, but he's rather traditional and expects obedience..." Her voice trailed off.

"I did get that impression." Silently, he cursed her father. She'd felt forced to accept him as a mate, seeing no other option. He tried to reassure her. "Our relationship has had a bit of an unusual start but I'll do my best to make you happy." Pausing, he wondered what else he could say or do to make this easier for her. "I need to check in with John to see what's happened while I was away, but after supper I'll take you for a walk around the immediate grounds. Then, tomorrow morning we can go for another run."

"I'd like that. It looks to be a nice territory." Elise twisted around so she could see out the window again.

He observed his land with pride. "It's a beautiful place, especially down by the lake. I think you'll enjoy it here, but just like at your old home, don't go too close to the edge of the property. We have the same problem with hunters and trappers that your old pack has."

She murmured her agreement but pressed her hand against the window pane, a sad look crossing her face.

He took her in his arms, running his hands down her back. "It will take some time to adjust, but soon this will feel like home. Don't worry. I'll be here to help you."

As he held Elise close, feeling her warmth and breathing in her scent, a sense of contentment settled within him, a new kind of happiness he hadn't experienced before. It felt right having her here, in his home, in his arms. Who would have thought when he'd first caught a glimpse of her months ago, that one day they'd end up mates? The hand of fate had definitely been involved.

For just a moment he allowed himself to dream. Everything in his life was finally falling into place. He was an Alpha, had a prosperous pack and a large territory. True, there were challenges to face but he'd handle them with his mate at his side. They'd blood-bond, have pups together, be a real family. The kind of family he never had, one filled with love, trust and respect.

Leaning back, he gazed down into Elise's eyes. She was young but she'd learn. He sensed an inner strength in her. Yes, the mating had been a good choice and he couldn't wait for what the future held for them.

Epilogue

Several years later...

"Kane? Kane!"

"Hmmm?" He frowned, tugged from sleep by the sound of Elise calling his name. Yawning, he opened his eyes and blinked at the brightness of the bedside lamp. A quick glance showed it was still dark outside, definitely not time to get up. "Is something wrong?"

Elise was propped up on one elbow, her hand on his chest. "That's what I want to know. You were mumbling to yourself, tossing and turning. It woke me up."

"Sorry." He rubbed his hand over his face. "I was dreaming."

"A good dream or a bad one?" She stroked his cheek, concern in her voice.

He turned to press his lips to her palm, her touch always affecting him. "A bit of both."

"Oh. Do you want to talk about it or is it top secret Alpha stuff?"

He chuckled. "You know there are no secrets between us."

"Just checking." She grinned at him.

"Sneaky wench." He pulled her closer so she was lying on top of him. "Did I mention I love that about you?"

"Not in so many words but there is definitely evidence to support your statement." She wiggled against him.

"Keep that up and we won't be getting back to sleep anytime soon."

"Well, if you're too tired..." Her voice trailed off as she began to slide off him but he held her in place.

"I'm never too tired for my mate." He flipped them over so she was pinned beneath him and then brushed the hair from her face and stared deeply into her eyes.

His love for her grew each day. She completed him, kept him grounded, balanced his sense of duty by reminding him he was more than just an Alpha. He was a father, a mate, a lover, a friend. He kissed her softly, tenderly, then with growing passion.

"The pups?" Elise pulled away.

He glanced at the door that separated their suite of rooms from their children's. Recently, his son had taken to getting up during the night. Some preventive measures seemed prudent.

"Just a minute." He left the bed and flicked the lock on the door.

"Good solution." Elise smiled her approval.

"I'm Alpha for a reason." He smirked as he joined her once again.

Soon they were lost in the throes of passion, the soft rustling of bedding, murmured words and stifled cries becoming the soundtrack of their love. Branding kisses and tender touches, gentle nips and masterful strokes; he brought them to trembling need before pausing. Her cheeks were flushed, her lips parted. He loved seeing her like this.

"You're so beautiful, Elise."

"And so are you." She reached up and tenderly brushed his hair from his forehead

"Alphas aren't beautiful. We're rugged, strong, tough..." He emphasized each word with a move that had her writhing.

"I change my mind. You're a teasing..." She paused and bit her lip, her fingers tightening their grip on his back in response to his skilled attention...

Afterwards, they drifted in a haze of satisfaction, enjoying the closeness that came after making love. Kane had tucked Elise close to his side and pulled up the covers to block the night chill.

"You never did tell me about your dream," Elise murmured as she drew an idle pattern on his chest.

"I didn't?" He gave a lop-sided grin. "You distracted me as I recall."

"Mmmm...It never takes much to *distract* you." She gave a soft laugh. "But the dream...?"

"It was about the first time I saw you."

"At my father's house? I remember walking into the room and seeing you. You were gorgeous with your dark hair and broad, muscular shoulders but the look you gave me..." She shivered. "It turned me into a nervous wreck!"

"Really? I didn't notice," he replied tongue-in-cheek. "But the fact is, I'd been fantasizing about you already."

"What do you mean?" She turned so she was looking him in the eye.

"I saw you at a movie theatre a few months earlier."

"You never told me that!"

He shrugged. "I hadn't thought about it for ages. For some reason my mind dredged it up tonight."

"Maybe it's that article Lycan Link wants to do about you."

"Could be."

"Well, whatever the reason, *I* want to hear the story first before it gets spread all over the world." She pinned him a stern look. "Spill the beans, Mr. Sinclair."

"Yes ma'am!" He gave her a mock salute, then hitched himself up against the headboard.

Giggling, she snuggled against his side.

He stared down at her, tracing her features with the tip of his finger, memories of a day long ago filling his mind once again. "It all started when I was at the movie theatre and saw the most beautiful girl in the world…"

~FIN~

A Message from Nicky

Hi!

Thanks so much for taking the time to read this novella. I actually had no plan to write this story until Mark Coker, CEO of Smashwords, suggested I add an extra little something to my planned release of the original trilogy in a boxed set. He said hard-core fans would want a little something more, some outtakes or deleted scenes.

I thought long and hard on his suggestion and then remembered how readers often asked for Kane's POV on The Mating and...well...this is the result!

If you enjoyed the story, please leave a review where you purchased it and/or send me an email. I love getting letters from my fans.

And in case you are wondering, there are a lot of characters and stories still stirring about in my imagination so stay tuned for more Law of the Lycans adventures!

~Nicky

Connect with Nicky Charles

Email me at
nicky.charles@live.ca

Visit my website:
http://www.nickycharles.com

Follow me on Facebook:
https://www.facebook.com/NickyCharles/

Books by Nicky Charles

Forever In Time

The Law of the Lycans series

The Mating
The Keeping
The Finding
Bonded
Betrayed: Days of the Rogue
Betrayed: Book 2 – The Road to Redemption
For the Good of All
Deceit can be Deadly
Kane: I am Alpha
Veil of Lies

Hearts & Halos
(Written with Jan Gordon)
In The Cards
Untried Heart

Lightning Source UK Ltd.
Milton Keynes UK
UKHW030057011021
391456UK00009B/1822